GIRL OF GLASS

Girl of Glass, Book One

MEGAN O'RUSSELL

Ink Worlds Press

Visit our website at www.MeganORussell.com

Girl of Glass

Cover Art by X Potion Designs (https://www.x-potion.net/)

Editing by Christopher Russell

Interior Design by Christopher Russell

Printed in the United States of America

DEDICATION

For Chris

GIRL OF GLASS

CHAPTER ONE

Nola dug her fingers into the warm dirt. Around her, the greenhouse smelled of damp earth, mist, and fresh, clean air.

Carefully, she took the tiny seed and placed it at the bottom of the hole her finger had made.

Thump.

Soon the seed would take root. A sprout would break through to the surface.

Thump, bang.

Then the green stem would grow until bean pods sprouted.

Bang, thump!

The food would be harvested and brought to their tables. All of the families would be fed.

"Ahhhhh!" the voice came from the other side of the glass. Nola knew she shouldn't look, but she couldn't ignore the sounds any longer.

It was a woman this time, her skin gray with angry, red patches dotting her face. She slammed her fists into the glass, leaving smears of red behind. The woman didn't seem to care as she banged her bloody hands into the glass over and over.

"Magnolia."

Nola jumped as Mrs. Pearson placed a hand on her shoulder.

"Don't pay her any mind," Mrs. Pearson said. "She can't get through the glass."

"But she's bleeding." Nola pushed the words past the knot in her throat.

The woman bashed her head against the glass.

"She needs help," Nola said. The woman stared right at her.

Mrs. Pearson took Nola's shoulders and turned her back to her plant tray. "That woman is beyond your help, Magnolia. Paying her any attention will only make it worse. There is nothing you can do."

Nola felt eyes staring at her. Not just the woman on the other side of the glass. The rest of the class was staring at her now, too.

Bang. Thump.

Families. The food she planted would feed the families.

Bang.

Pop.

Nola spun back to the glass. Two guards were outside now. One held his gun high. A thin spike protruded from the woman's neck. Her eyelids fluttered for a moment before she slid down the glass, leaving a streak of blood behind her.

"See," Mrs. Pearson said, smoothing Nola's hair, "they'll take her where she can't hurt herself or any of us ever again."

Nola nodded, turning back to the tray of dirt. Make a hole, plant the seed, grow the food. But the streaks of blood were burned into her mind.

The setting sun gave the greenhouse an orange-red gleam when the chime finally sounded.

"Students," Mrs. Pearson called over the sounds of her class packing up for the evening, "remember, tomorrow is Charity Day. Please dress and prepare accordingly. Anyone who doesn't come ready to leave the domes will be sent home, and their grades will be docked."

"Thank you, Mrs. Pearson," the students chorused as they drifted down into the hall.

"Magnolia."

Nola pretended she hadn't heard Mrs. Pearson call her name as she slipped in front of the group leaving the greenhouse. She didn't want to be asked if she was all right or told the sick woman would be cared for. And she didn't want to see if the glass had already been wiped clean.

Lights flickered on, sensing the group heading down the steps. Hooks lined the hallway, awaiting the gardening uniforms. Nola pulled off her rubber boots and unzipped her brown and green jumpsuit, straightening her sweater before shrugging out of the dirt-covered uniform. The rest of the class chatted as they changed—plans for the evening, talk of tomorrow's trip into the city. Nola beat the rest of them to the sink to scrub her hands. The harsh smell of the soap stung her nose, and the steaming water turned her hands red. But in a minute, the only sign of her time in the greenhouses that remained was a bit of dirt on the long brown braid that hung over her shoulder.

"Nola." Jeremy Ridgeway took his place next to Nola at the sinks, shaking the dirt from his light brown hair like a dog. It would have been funny if Nola had been in the mood to laugh. "Are you ready for tomorrow?"

"Sure. It's our duty to help the less fortunate." She sounded like a parrot, repeating what their teachers said every time Charity Day came around. Nola turned to walk away.

Jeremy stopped her, taking her hand.

"Are you okay?" Wrinkles formed on his forehead, and concern filled his deep brown eyes.

"Of course." Nola forced herself to smile.

"Do you want to come over tonight?" Jeremy asked, still holding her hand. "I mean"—his cheeks flushed—"my sister and my dad are off-duty tonight, and she hasn't seen you in a while."

"I've got to get home. My mom leaves tomorrow. But tell your dad and Gentry I said hi." Nola pulled her hand away and half-ran down the hall. More lights flickered on as she sped down the corridor. She made herself breathe, fighting her guilt at running away from Jeremy. She liked being in the greenhouses better than the tunnels that dug down into the earth. There might only be a few feet of dirt on top of her, but knowing it was there pressed an impossible weight on her lungs.

The hum of the air-filtration system calmly buzzed overhead. The solar panels aboveground generated power so she could breathe down here. She pictured the schematics in her head. Lots of vents. Great big vents. The air would be filtered, cleaned and purified, and the big vents would bring oxygen down to her.

Blue paint on the wall read *Bright Dome* above an arrow pointing to a corridor on the left. Nola ran faster, knowing soon she would be aboveground. In a minute she was sprinting up the steps. She took a deep, gulping breath. The air in the tunnels might be the same as the air in the domes, but it felt so different.

The sun had set, leaving only the bright lights of the city across the river and the faint twinkle of the other domes to peer through the glass. Nola squinted at the far side of Bright Dome. The other homestead domes glowed gently, but if she tried, she could almost make out a few stars. At least that's what she told herself. It might only have been wishful thinking.

Tall trees reached almost to the roof of Bright Dome. Grass and wildflowers coated the ground around the stone footpaths that led from house to house. Nola followed the path through the buildings to the far side of the dome. Twelve families shared Bright Dome, each of them lucky enough to have been granted independent housing units.

The trees in the dome hung heavy with crisp, green leaves. The flowers had begun to close their petals for the night. A squirrel darted past Nola's feet.

"A little late getting home, buddy." Nola's pulse slowed with each step closer to home.

The birds were all flying back to their nests. Bright Dome had been assigned robins and blue jays this cycle. The birds and the squirrels shared their home to be kept safe from contamination. The domes provided them all protection from the toxic air and tainted water.

The lights were on in Nola's house as she swung open the door.

"Hey, Mom," Nola called.

"Mmmmhmmm." The sound came from her mother's office in the back of the kitchen.

"How was your day?" Nola pulled the pot of steaming vegetables from the stove, knowing they would be overdone without having to lift the lid.

"Fine," her mother said, running her fingers through her shoulder-length, chestnut hair, which had been graying quickly of late. "We've been running samples in the lab all day."

"You'll figure it out." Nola didn't ask what the problem in the lab was. Her mother, Lenora Kent, was one of the heads of the botanical preservation group. It was their job to decide what plants from the outside needed to be preserved and how to take care of those plants once they were safely inside the domes. Whatever her mother was working on was for the good of them all. Beyond that it was all vague answers about classified projects.

Nola pulled bowls down from the cabinet, dishing out steamed beans and broccoli, adding spices to make the food taste like something real.

Nola pushed the bowl in front of her mother. Only when she put the spoon in Lenora's hand did her mother seem to notice Nola was still in the room.

"How was your day, sweetie?" Lenora looked up at her daughter.

Nola's mind flashed to the woman. Pounding on the glass, shattering the serenity of the greenhouse.

"It was fine." Nola smiled. "Don't forget to pack for the conference. It'll be colder at Green Leaf, so pack your sweaters."

"Of course." Lenora nodded, but she was already looking back at the charts on her computer screen.

Nola carried her dinner up the narrow stairs to the second floor. She crept into her mother's room and found the duffel bag under her bed. Nola pulled clothes out of the tiny closet. They were lucky. The residents of the domes hadn't been forced into uniforms outside of work and school. Yet. That would come when there was no one left on the outside to work in manufacturing.

When she had counted out enough blouses and slacks for her mother's week-long trip, Nola moved the suitcase to the head of the bed, where her mother would have to see it if she went to sleep that night. A picture in a carved wood frame sat on the nightstand. Six faces beamed out of the photo. A ten-year-old version of herself sat in a tree above her mother and father. Kieran sat on the branch next to her, and below him were his parents.

Nola touched her father's face, wishing the photo was larger so she could properly see his bright blue eyes that had matched her own. But her father was dead, killed in the same riot as Kieran's mother. And now Kieran and his father had been banished from the domes. The photo blurred as tears pooled in Nola's eyes.

She slid the picture into the top of her mother's bag. Lenora would need a bit of home during the Green Leaf Conference—even if their family had broken.

Nola snuck across the tiny landing at the top of the stairs and into her room. She climbed straight into bed, leaving her dinner forgotten on her desk. She pushed her face into her pillow, hoping sleep would come before the face of the woman desperate to get through the glass.

CHAPTER TWO

The scent of stale vegetables filled Nola's room when her lights flickered on the next morning. A faint beeping came before the computerized voice that said, "Reminder: today is Charity Day. Please dress in uniform, remember sun protection, pack I-Vent..."

"Yeah, yeah." Nola rubbed her eyes.

"Remember," the computer continued, "charity must be done to ease the suffering of those on the outside, but protecting yourself means the salvation of mankind."

"I said, I got it!" Nola tossed her shoe at the wall.

Her mother's bedroom door was open, and the kitchen was empty. "Have fun at your conference, Mom," Nola muttered to the empty house as she ran out the door.

It was easier to go through the tunnels in the morning, when she knew sunlight filled the domes above, but still, Nola walked as quickly as she could without being glared at by the people she passed.

The bus into the city would leave from the atrium, the only place in the domes with an exit to the outside world. Five-minute walk underground, then in the outside for four hours, then class, then to the greenhouses. Nola made the list in her mind.

Not too bad. I can get through today.

"Nola!" a voice called from behind her.

Nola slowed her step without looking back.

A moment later, Jeremy walked at her side.

"You ready for this?" Jeremy's voice bounced with excitement.

"Yep." Nola held up her wide brim hat and gloves before patting the I-Vent in her back pocket. "Ready for a trip into the dangerous world. How could I not be with PAM's help this morning?"

"So, your computer got a little snarky with you, too?" Jeremy smiled. "I love how it gives us the 'greater good' speech before we go out and try to help people."

Nola shrugged. She wanted to say, *How much good do you think doling out one meal a month to the people we deem worthy of our assistance really does?* But Jeremy looked so hopeful she couldn't bear to disillusion him before they had to look the outsiders in the face.

"If we get on the bus soon enough, we can call the good jobs." Jeremy took her hand and pulled her, running down the corridor.

Nola laughed as she tried to keep up, her voice echoing through the hall. People turned to stare at them, but that only made Jeremy run faster.

Nola's step faltered as she tried to keep up with Jeremy's much longer stride. She laughed through her panting breath as they rounded a corner and darted past a group of their classmates.

"Last one to the bus scrubs the pans!" Jeremy shouted.

The green bus waited for them in the atrium. Mr. Pillion shook his head but didn't bother hiding his smile as they skidded to a stop in front of the bus.

"Morning." Nola pinched the stitch in her side.

"Good morning, Magnolia. Jeremy." Mr. Pillion's puffy white hair bounced as he nodded.

Nola bit her lip. He always reminded her of one of the snowy white sheep from the Farm Dome. Images of the farm workers sheering Mr. Pillion's hair floated through her mind.

"I'd like to take ladle duty." Jeremy turned to Nola.

Nola didn't really care what job she had. Being out there and seeing the outsiders was terrible. Did it really matter if she scrubbed pans, too? But Jeremy stared at her, eyebrows raised.

"Ladle for me, too, please," Nola said.

Jeremy smiled and moved to pull Nola onto the bus.

"Wait," Mr. Pillion said, holding out a hand. "One dose each from the I-Vent before we get on the bus."

"But we don't use them till we're on the road," Nola said.

The I-Vents cleared their lungs of the smog that hung heavy over the city. There was no reason to use them in the pure air of the domes.

"There was a riot last night." Mr Pillion's usually cheerful face darkened. "There's still smoke in the air, so we need to be more cautious."

Nola pulled the I-Vent from her back pocket. Holding the metal cylinder to her lips, she took one deep breath, letting the vapor pour over her tongue. The medicine tasted metallic and foul. She shivered as the mist chilled her throat. Nola pictured the drugs working. Finding all of the impurities in her lungs and rooting them out. Forming a protective layer to keep the toxins from seeping deep into the tissue.

"Good." Mr. Pillion nodded, lowering his arm and allowing them onto the bus.

A line of other students had formed behind them now.

"Everyone. One puff of the I-Vent before you can get on the bus," Mr. Pillion called to the crowd. "No, Nikki, you cannot get on the bus without your hat."

"That girl is going to fail again this year," Jeremy whispered as a girl with bright blond hair ran back to the tunnels.

A few of their classmates had beaten them onto the bus. Their class was for ages fifteen through eighteen. Some aged into the next group before others, but really they had been together since they were little, the younger ones rejoining the older ones when they moved to the next age level. They had all split into groups of friends years ago, and nothing had changed besides their heights. Until Kieran left.

"Nola," Jeremy said, offering Nola the seat next to his.

She should be sitting next to Kieran.

If he were still here.

Lilly, Nikki's best friend, raised an eyebrow and tilted her head toward the open seat next to her.

"Sure." Nola smiled at Jeremy.

Lilly winked, giving Nola a sly grin before turning back to her book.

Nola sat down next to Jeremy. He leaned casually against the wire-laced window, watching the other students loading onto the bus. Nola's chest hummed. She kept her gaze on her hands, afraid Jeremy would hear her heart racing. How could he look so calm and handsome when they were about to leave the domes?

"Everyone ready?" Mr. Pillion asked.

"Yes, sir," the class chorused.

"Good." Mr. Pillion took his seat. Eight guards in full riot gear loaded onto the bus, sitting up front by the door.

"Umm, Mr. Pillion," Lilly said, "are you sure we should be going out there if we need eight guards?"

They always had guards when they went out for Charity Day. But usually only four, and never in full riot gear.

"We cannot allow the unfortunate actions of a few to dissuade us from helping the many," Mr. Pillion said as the bus pulled up to the giant, metal bay doors. "We must show the population we are here to assist and protect them as long as they remain law-abiding citizens. I promise you we have done everything possible to ensure your safety."

A low rumble shook the bus roof as the atrium ventilation

system prepared for the bay doors to open. Nola's ears popped as a *whoosh* flowed through the bus. She pinched her nose and pushed air into her ears along with the rest of the class.

The metal door scraped open, and unfiltered sunlight poured in. Guards in uniforms and masks stood at attention outside the dome doors, their gaze sweeping the horizon for unseen threats.

"What happened last night?" Nola whispered to Jeremy.

"A bunch of Vampers," Jeremy muttered. The people in the seats around them leaned in. "They're ridiculous. They take a bunch of drugs that make them crazy then cause trouble for the poor people who are just trying to survive."

"I've heard the Vampers are invincible," Rayland said, his pudgy face pale with fright.

"They aren't invincible." Jeremy shook his head. "My dad's Captain of the Outer Guard, so I've heard more about the Vampers than you could come up with in your nightmares. And my dad's people have taken them down before."

"But what about last night?" Lilly said.

"The Outer Guard went in to raid one of the Vamp labs," Jeremy said. "It got messy."

"I heard," Lilly said, shivering as she spoke, "Vampers actually drink blood. I don't think I could fight a person who drank blood. It would be like offering them a buffet of you."

"Vampers aren't people." Disgust twisted Jeremy's face.

"Why would they drink blood?" Nola swallowed the bile rising in her throat.

"Because they're a bunch of sickos," Jeremy spat. "And they're taking the city down with them. The rest of the neighborhood around the Vamp lab freaked out, like the guards were stealing food from orphans, and the riot started. They burned down a whole block before the guards could stop it."

"Were any of the guards hurt?" Nola's balled her hands into tight fists, hiding their trembling.

"No." Jeremy took her hands in his. "All of our people are fine."

"I get that life out there is a nightmare," Lilly said, sliding back to her own seat, "but why would they try to make it worse?"

Nola looked out the window, watching as they crossed the long bridge into the city. Children ran barefoot on the sidewalks, their heads exposed to the pounding sun. Garbage had been tossed along the curb, bringing insects and wild animals to feast on the refuse. Even with the ventilation system on the bus, the stench of stagnant water and the sickening sweetness of rotting fruit tainted the air.

Jeremy squeezed her hands tighter as he followed her gaze out the window.

It was easy to forget the world was ending when you lived in the safety of the domes.

CHAPTER THREE

When they were only a few blocks from the Charity Center, a video screen folded down from the ceiling at the front of the bus.

"Are you ready for this?" Jeremy snuck past Nola to kneel in the center of the aisle, facing the rest of the students.

Jeremy coughed as the screen blinked to life.

"Jeremy," Mr. Pillion said in a warning tone.

"I'm word-perfect, sir," Jeremy said. "They will receive all the dire warnings accurately."

A man appeared on the screen, and Jeremy turned back to the class, plastering a somber look on his face to match the man in the video.

"Good morning, students," Jeremy said with the man on the screen.

"Good morning, Jeremy," the class echoed.

Jeremy smiled and nodded in perfect sync with the man.

"As we near the Charity Center, please take a moment to utilize your I-Vents." The man lifted a shiny, silver tube to his mouth and took an exaggerated breath.

Sounds of squeaking seats and pockets unzipping floated

through the bus as the students dug out their I-Vents to follow suit.

"Good," Jeremy said with the man on the screen. "Remember, it only takes one day of soiled air to begin contaminating the lungs." Jeremy faked a cough before continuing with the video. "Your work today is important. While we within the domes work hard to live a healthy life, the people in this city do not have the opportunities for safety and security that we do. Poverty is rampant, and sometimes even simple things like food are unattainable."

Jeremy dropped face-first onto the floor as the screen switched to a video of orphans, sitting at a long table, their young faces sad and drawn. Even as they ate, hunger filled their sunken eyes.

The screen changed back to the man, and Jeremy popped up to his knees.

"Poverty can induce desperation." Jeremy placed both pointer fingers on his chin, his hands clasped together. "To ensure your safety while helping the needy, here are a few simple rules to follow: First, do not leave the Charity Center or the perimeter secured by the guards."

The guards at the front of the bus waved, earning a laugh from the students.

"Second, do not partake in the food we are here to provide the less fortunate. The food provided is for them, not for the people of the domes. Third, an unfortunate side effect of living in the sad conditions of the city is an insurgence of drug use among the desperate." A new face appeared on the screen. The man's eyes were bloodshot almost to the point of his irises being red. Red splotches marked the pale skin of his cheeks. "Everyone who enters the Charity Center must submit to testing to ensure no drugs are present in their systems. However, should an addict—"

"Vamper!" the students shouted together, laughing at their own joke.

But the image of the woman beating on the glass flew unbidden into Nola's mind. She dug her nails into her palms as the man on the screen, and Jeremy, kept talking.

"—attempt to enter the Charity Center, approach the bus as you enter or exit the Charity Center, or in any way harass you, alert the guards immediately. Though a user may seem normal and calm, they could become violent at any moment. While helping those who live on the outside is important, above all, we must consider—"

"The safety of the domes!" the class chanted together as the bus rumbled to a stop outside an old stone building.

The doors opened, and the eight guards piled out. The students stood, all cramming into the aisle, ready to get off the bus.

"Did you like my dramatic interpretation?" Jeremy asked.

Nola nodded, pulling on her sunhat and trying to stay in step as everyone moved off the bus.

The Charity Center was dark gray, almost black stone. But in a few places the black had been worn away in long tear-like streaks, showing the rosy brown color the building had been before years of filth had built up on it. Iron bars strong enough to keep rioters away from the charity supplies crisscrossed the closed windows.

The class filed up the chipped stone steps. The guards flanked the stairs, their gaze sweeping the streets.

How terrible was the riot to make the best of us afraid?

Jeremy leaned into Nola and whispered, "Two more."

"What?" Nola said, trying not to gag as the smell of harsh cleaners and mass produced food flooded her nose.

"I turn eighteen in two months." Jeremy smiled as they filed into the changing room. Aprons and gloves had been laid out for each of the students. "Eighteen means I graduate and go to trade training. Eighteen means no more Charity Days. I only have to do this two more times."

Nola counted. Eleven months. Eleven more times she would

have to look into the eyes of hungry people and know that, though she was feeding them today, tomorrow they would be hungry again. And while they suffered, she would be locked safely back in the domes. With fresh food and clean air.

Jeremy pulled on his gloves with a sharp *snap*. "Let's do this."

It took an hour to heat all the food in the giant kitchens. Old stoves and ovens lined one wall, their surfaces covered in years of built up grease and grime that refused to be cleaned. Shelves of chipped trays and bent utensils loomed over the giant sinks that hummed as the dome-made filters cleaned the water before the students were allowed to wash their hands.

Years of repetition had trained the class in how to get the work done as quickly as possible. One group prepped the giant pots and pans as another group pulled great sacks of flour and milled corn down from the shelves.

Nola and Lilly went into a hallway in the back.

Large cans of food lined the corridor. In the dim, flickering light, Nola had to squint to read the labels to find the cans they needed.

Stewed beets and black beans.

"Can you believe they think this is food?" Lilly shook her head, loading as many cans into her arms as she could carry. "How old is this stuff?"

Nola watched Lilly's silhouette waddle awkwardly down the hall before loading cans of processed fruit into her arms and following.

An iron-barred window bled light into the back of the kitchen. Nola peered through the soot-streaked glass. The line of people waiting to be fed wound around the block.

"What's out there?" Wrinkles formed between Mr. Pillion's white eyebrows as he squinted out the window.

"I've never seen that many people waiting before." Nola tightened her grip on the cans as they slipped.

"A good number of people lost their homes last night." Mr.

Pillion shrugged before turning to the rest of the class and shouting, "We open the doors in five minutes!"

The trays and pots of food were moved to the serving room as the doors opened.

The first in line was a woman with two little boys behind her.

"Hand," the guard said, though the woman already had her hand held up as though she were carrying a tray.

The guard held a small black rectangle over the woman's palm. She winced as the needle pierced her skin. The device glowed green, and the woman lifted her older son, who bit his lip as the black box tested his blood, immediately flashing the green light. The smaller boy couldn't have been more than three. He buried his face in his mother's shoulder as the guard tested him for the drugs that ran rampant in the city. The little boy pulled his hand away and held it close to his chest as the guard waited for the light.

Nola hadn't realized she was holding her breath until the guard said, "Enjoy your meal," as the light flashed green, clearing the small boy.

The mother handed each of the boys a tray before picking one up for herself. Nola watched as they came down the line. Each of the ladle workers doled out portions of whatever was in their pot. Nola looked down at the green and brown slop as she scooped it onto the small boy's plate. She didn't even know exactly what she was serving him.

He paused in front of Nola. Purple rings marked his face under his big brown eyes. His lungs rattled as he took a breath to mutter, "Thank you."

A fist closed around Nola's heart. She wanted to stop the line. To find a way to help the poor boy with the bad lungs. But he had already walked away, pushed forward by his brother, and his mother, and the long line of other hungry people wanting food.

Nola worked mechanically, staring at the little boy until his mother took him out the heavy wooden door at the far end of the room, clearing seats so more could eat. But the line still hadn't stopped. Nola's ladle scraped the bottom of the pot.

She'd run out of food. And judging by the angry murmurs rising from the front of the line, she wasn't the only one.

"Go get more cans," Mr. Pillion whispered in Nola's ear. "I don't care what it is. Get cans, mix it together, and put it in a pot."

A man at the back of the line shoved people out of the way, trying to get to the food before it disappeared.

With a *hiss* and a *pop*, one of the guards shot the man in the neck with a tiny needle that disappeared into his flesh, leaving only a glint of silver at the top of a trickle of red.

The crowd screamed as more people began to push.

"Go. Now." Mr. Pillion scrambled up onto the counter. "Please remain calm! We are going to start making more food immediately. Everyone in line will be fed, but we must ask for your patience."

Nola slipped into the kitchen as the crowd began to shout over Mr. Pillion's voice.

CHAPTER FOUR

The darkness of the storage hall had never bothered her before. But the echoing shouts from the dining room, from people who could have been a part of the riot, transformed each shadow she passed into a person waiting to attack.

"Get it together, Nola." She grabbed cans down from the shelves.

She stumbled under their weight as she ran back to the kitchen and shoved the armload of cans onto the counter. Shouts carried from the serving room. The angry voices of the crowd drowned out Mr. Pillion. Nola sprinted back into the storeroom, reached up to the top self, and pulled down giant cans of beans.

"Nola."

Pain shot up her leg as the heavy can dropped onto her foot.

"Careful now," the voice came again.

Nola spun around.

A pale boy with dark hair and green eyes flecked with gold smiled at her.

"Kieran," Nola gasped, running to him and throwing her arms around his neck, all thoughts of food and riots forgotten.

He had changed since the last time she had seen him nearly a year ago. Muscles had filled out his lanky frame, and his hair had grown longer, hanging over his ears.

"What are you doing here?" Nola stepped back, looking into his face.

"It's Charity Day." Kieran shrugged, his smile fading.

Nola's stomach dropped. "Are you here for food? Are things that bad?" She thought of Kieran's father, a man so brilliant simple things like eating had always seemed trivial to him.

A man like him shouldn't be on the streets.

Kieran shook his head. "Dad and I are fine. I know this may shock you, but getting kicked out of the domes didn't kill either of us."

"Kieran—"

"Dad's still working in medical research, but now instead of being told only to help the elite and getting thrown out for trying to help people who really need it—"

"That's not—"

"People out here love him," Kieran said, his voice suddenly crisp and hostile. "Out here, he saves people."

"He's brilliant," Nola said. "He's been saving people as long as I've known him."

A smile flickered across Kieran's face. "We're doing good." Kieran took Nola's hand. Calluses covered his cold palms.

"If you're doing well, then why are you here?" Nola asked. She had been in the storage room for too long. Someone would come looking for her soon.

Unless the dining room's turned into a riot.

"I came to see you." Kieran brushed a stray curl away from her cheek. "I don't need contaminated food dished out by Domers."

"The food isn't contaminated," Nola said, trying to ignore her racing heart and Kieran's tone when he said *Domers.*

"Then why aren't you allowed to eat it?" Kieran asked.

"Because it's for the poor."

"Someday you won't be able to believe that."

He reached across the few inches between them, sliding his hand from her shoulder to her cheek.

"I need your I-Vent," he whispered.

"You're sick?" The butterflies in her stomach disappeared, replaced by the sting of panic.

"I'm fine," Kieran said. "It's not for me."

"I can't give medicine out." Nola took a step back, shaking her head. "I'm not allowed to distribute resources."

"They have stores of medicine in the domes," Kieran said. "I only need one."

"If I give you medicine and they find out..." Kieran's father was important, a savior to the domes, and they cast him out for giving away the community's food.

I'd be banished before sundown.

"I can't do that."

"Tell them it was stolen." Kieran stepped forward, closing the distance between them. "Tell them I did it." He wrapped his arms around her, pulling her close.

Nola's heart pounded in her ears. His face was a breath from hers. His hands on her waist. The cold of his fingers cut through her sweater as he traced the line of her hips.

He pressed his lips to her forehead. "Thank you, Nola."

She raised her lips to meet his, but Kieran stepped back, holding out his hand. Her I-Vent rested in his palm.

"You're saving a life."

He turned and strode away, disappearing into the darkness before the tears formed in her eyes.

Nola stood alone in the dark.

She could scream. She *should* scream. She should shout to the guards that an outsider had stolen dome medicine. But would they be able to hear her over the chaos in the dining room? And what if they caught Kieran? Would they shoot a tiny, silver needle into his neck?

She grabbed a few cans without reading the contents and ran

back to the kitchen. Her whole class stood in the back of the room, craning their necks to look out the window.

"I can't believe they thought they could get away with that," Jeremy growled. He was taller than most of the class and had a clear view of the street below.

"What happened?" Nola stood on her tiptoes, trying to see over the heads of her classmates.

"After they neutralized the first guy, people got crazy," Jeremy said. "More people started shouting. Then people were pushing to get to the food. Mr. Pillion got knocked off the counter. Then the guards took a few more people down, and everyone else just sort of ran away."

"It was terrible." Lilly's voice wavered. Marco wrapped an arm around her, and Lilly turned to cry into his shoulder.

Mr. Pillion burst through the doors to the kitchen. "Everyone back on the bus, now."

Nola turned to go back to the hall to put the cans away.

"Leave it, Magnolia!" Mr. Pillion said.

Jeremy grabbed the heavy cans from her and tossed them onto a table before grabbing Nola's hand and dragging her back through the door they had come in less than two hours before.

Only two guards joined them as the students scrambled to their seats. The door shut, and the bus jerked forward.

Nola stumbled and Jeremy caught her, holding her close as they drove away.

Groups of people lined the sidewalk. Whether they had been in the Charity Center or only come to see what the commotion was, Nola didn't know.

A terrible *crunch* sounded from the front of the bus as a brick hit the windshield, leaving a mark like a spider web in the glass. The bus accelerated as the shouts of the crowd grew.

They reached the outskirts of the city. The domes rose in the distance, shining across the river, high in the hills.

"Class," Mr. Pillion said, holding a hand over his heart as he spoke, "our world is falling apart. It has been for a long time. The greatest trial of those who survive is to watch the continuous decay that surrounds them. As the outside world grows worse, so too does the plight of the city dwellers. We witnessed the desperation that plight is causing today. Let us not dwell on the harm they might have done to us. Rather, let us be grateful for all we have. For if our roles were reversed, I promise you each of us would be as desperate as those we saw today." He took his I-Vent from his shirt pocket and held the silver tip to his lips, taking a deep breath. "We must be grateful for even the simplest of things."

Mr. Pillion sat, and the students dug through their pockets for their I-Vents.

Jeremy took a deep breath from his before turning to Nola.

She stared down at her hands, willing Jeremy not to look at her. There were scratches on her fingers. How had she gotten them?

"You need to do your I-Vent." Jeremy nudged Nola.

"I lost mine," Nola whispered, "I—" Jeremy had known Kieran. They had been friends. But Kieran wasn't one of them anymore. "I think it fell out of my pocket when things got crazy."

"Use mine." Jeremy pressed the silver tube into her palm.

Nola stared down at it. Kieran had come to find her for a tiny tube.

To save a life.

"Look, don't be nervous about asking for a new one," Jeremy murmured into Nola's ear, wrapping his arm around her. "I'll go with you. And after what happened today, I don't think anyone is going to blame you for losing it."

"Right." Nola gave a smile she hoped looked real before holding the tube up to her lips and waiting for the metallic taste to fill her mouth.

CHAPTER FIVE

Nola flopped down in bed.

It had taken hours to get a new I-Vent from the medical department. There were forms to fill out and questions to answer. Jeremy had wanted to stay with her to keep her company, but the doctor kicked him out. A quick "See you tomorrow!" was all he managed to say before the door *swooshed* shut in front of him.

They drew blood and performed a chest scan to be sure she hadn't been skipping her doses. Nola was too tired to argue that she hadn't been skipping anything. That she had used Jeremy's I-Vent on the way back from the Charity Center.

After a few hours, the doctor finally declared her lungs undamaged and gave her a new I-Vent. None of them seemed to suspect the old one had been stolen. And no one mentioned Kieran Wynne.

Nola lay on her back, staring at the new I-Vent in her hand. She held it up, watching the light reflect off its silver surface.

Such a simple thing.

Medicine in a tube. But Kieran needed it to save someone.

Nola dug her fists into her eyes, trying to wipe away the thoughts of Dr. Wynne ill. Or Kieran himself.

It's just a little tube.

She had been carrying one in her back pocket every time she left the domes for as long as she could remember. Was that why Kieran had come to her, because he knew where she kept her I-Vent? Or had he simply been waiting in the darkness for one of the students to be alone?

Her skin tingled where he'd held her hips, pulling her close. All he had wanted was a chance to steal the I-Vent.

How had she not felt him take it? Was she that mesmerized by seeing him again?

Nola shoved her hand in her back pocket. Her fingers found something crisp. She pulled out a piece of yellowed, folded up paper.

Nola

Her name was written on the paper in Kieran's untidy scrawl. She recognized the careless way he swished his pen. Her hands shook as she unfolded the note.

Dear Nola,

I'm sorry I had to get you involved in all this. I needed the medicine, and I had a feeling you wouldn't turn me in. If you knew the girl who needed it, you wouldn't be angry at all. She's sick, Nola. Lots of people out here are. I know I can't save everyone right now, but I need to start with her.

I wish you could meet her. I only hope the I-Vent can buy her some more time. I wish I could repay you. If you ever need me, the folks at 5th and Nightland know how to find me.

I miss you, Nola.

Please forgive me,

Kieran

. . .

Nola buried her face in her pillow. He had planned to see her. He had written a note for her.

He came for me.

She couldn't breathe. The pure air of the domes crushed her lungs. Nola's heart raced. The energy pulsing through her veins begged her to run away or break through the glass. She opened her bedroom window and climbed up onto the sill. With a practiced motion, she grabbed the groove at the edge of the roofline and, using the wall for support, pulled herself up onto the soft moss that covered the roof. She lay down, taking deep, shuddering breaths. Her arms stung from pulling herself up, but she was grateful for the ache. The sting took her mind off her racing heart. And Kieran.

If you ever need me.

What would she need him for? He was an outsider. A city dweller. She had everything she needed in the domes.

Everything but him.

She dug her fingers into the moss. The thin layer of dirt beneath still held the heat of the day. Kieran had known her better than anyone. He had been her best friend. They had held hands, supporting each other at her father and his mother's funerals.

He was the only boy she'd ever kissed.

Three faint beeps echoed throughout the dome. Then there was a little *pop* and a *hiss* as the rain system turned on.

The cool water spattered her skin. Nola didn't move as it soaked her. If she lay there long enough, would she disappear into the soft moss of the roof?

The dome-made rain drenched Kieran's letter, washing the ink away. Nola tore the letter into sopping pieces and let them dissolve with the rain. No one could see that letter. No one could know she had seen him.

5th and Nightland. That was all she needed.

"One of the most elementary lessons farmers learned early on was crop rotation." Mrs. Pearson drew the words on the wall with her silver pen. "Why is crop rotation so important?"

Nikki's hand shot up in the air.

Mrs. Pearson's eyebrows arched high. "Yes, Nikki?"

"You have to change what crops you grow where so you don't exhaust the soil," Nikki said.

"Very good," Mrs. Pearson said.

The concept of crop rotation was something they covered every year. Just like studying the importance of the ozone when the summer heat scorched the city beyond the glass—an inescapable measure of the passing of another year.

Mrs. Pearson slid her hand on the wall, and the words she had written flew away. She began to scrawl out equations. Tapping the corner of the wall, pictures of plants and soil sprung up around the border of the screen.

Nola let her mind wander, staring out the tiny window in the corner. She knew the equations. She knew how to test the soil and how to make it fertile again. Her mother had been training her to join the Botanical Preservation Group for years. Some kids got to choose which branch of the domes they wanted to work in once they turned eighteen and finished school. Nola had known her path since she was a little girl.

Her eyelids grew heavy. She hadn't been able to sleep last night. Hadn't been able to keep thoughts of Kieran from racing through her mind. What if he needed her?

What if I need him?

The bell beeped softly in the corner. As one, the class stood, putting their tablets back into their bags.

"Nola," Mrs. Pearson called as Nola reached the door to the hall.

Nola gritted her teeth and turned around.

"I wanted you to know I spoke with your mother over the com system yesterday," Mrs. Pearson said, her tone serious as she folded her hands in front of her.

"My mother?" Nola asked. "What happened? Why did she call?"

"We were discussing the progress of the Green Leaf Conference, and the topic of the incident at the Charity Center came up," Mrs. Pearson continued. "You reacted so poorly to the unfortunate woman outside the Green Dome, and then to have another shock so near after..." Mrs. Pearson pursed her lips, giving Nola a pitying look, like she was ill. Like there was something wrong with her, Nola, for being upset.

"I'm fine." Nola pushed her face into a smile.

"After losing your father—"

"That was three years ago," Nola cut across. "I'm fine."

Nola turned and walked out of the room, ignoring Mrs. Pearson calling after her.

As she turned into the hall, a hand caught her arm. Nola gasped as Jeremy fell into step beside her. "Don't scare me like that."

"You all right?" he asked.

"Why does everyone think I'm not okay today?" Nola twisted her arm away from Jeremy.

"Maybe it's the full moon." Jeremy took Nola by the shoulders, turning her to face him. "Maybe you're a member of one of the new packs."

Nola caught herself smiling a little. "Pack of what? Did the wildlife department bring in coyotes?" Nola rubbed a hand over her face. "I mean, I get we're the new Ark and we're supposed to preserve living creatures in a dying world and all, but I still think the insect habitats are creepy. And now they want to bring in coyotes?"

"I never said anything about coyotes. It's the new big thing in the city. I was talking to my dad about it."

"So, pack of what then?" Nola asked.

Jeremy draped an arm around her shoulders and started walking slowly down the hall. He spoke in a low voice as though telling a frightening bedtime story. "Werewolves. It's the new drug craze. Lycan. Outsiders have started injecting it."

"Isn't Vamp bad enough?" Nola shuddered. "Exactly how many drugs do people need? And why would they risk taking something that dangerous?" The woman outside Green Dome flashed through Nola's mind. Fighting to get through the glass, seeking out flesh to tear with no thought left for anything else. A zombie.

Jeremy shrugged. "This one is different. It makes you stronger, faster. You heal more quickly."

"Just like Vamp," Nola murmured.

"But Lycan changes your pheromones. The riot two nights ago. The guards tried to arrest a man for prowling around during the raid on the Vamp lab. Turns out he was the alpha of one of the packs."

"Like wolves."

"Just like wolves," Jeremy said, his voice shifting from conspiratorial to angry. "And when the pack found out the guards had their Alpha, they attacked. They're the ones who lit that building on fire. It destroyed a whole block, and the guards had to kill a few of them just to get away."

Vampires, zombies, and now werewolves.

A thousand horrible images of blood and fear tumbled through Nola's mind.

"So, they're still out there?" Nola asked, wishing she were aboveground, not just so she didn't feel like she were being crushed by the earth, but to be able to see out the glass—to be able to see if the wolves were coming.

And to escape.

"For now," Jeremy said.

Nola stared at Jeremy's face, trying to see the color of his eyes instead of streets painted red with blood.

"How do you know any of this?" Nola asked.

"My father," Jeremy said.

"Why did he tell you?" Nola asked. "You're always complaining he doesn't tell you anything about what he does outside."

His father was the head of the Outer Guard who patrolled the city. What they did, most people didn't want to know about.

"Because"—Jeremy paused, stepping forward to face Nola—"I just found out that, as of my birthday, I'll be training to join the Outer Guard."

"What?"

"Dad told me." Jeremy beamed. "It's everything I want."

"That's amazing!" Nola stood on her toes and threw her arms around Jeremy's neck. He pulled her in close, his chest rumbling against hers as he laughed.

"He's been telling me things so I'll be up on all the business of the city when I start training," Jeremy said. "Just don't tell anyone. About the Outer Guard or the wolves. The 'guard' thing won't be announced until next month, and my dad doesn't want people freaking out about the werewolves."

"Why would they want to be called that?" Nola shivered.

"When I get one, I'll ask." Jeremy winked. "But don't worry about them." Jeremy took Nola's hand, pulling her more quickly down the hall, almost running in his excitement. "We're safe here. No one can get into the domes. There isn't a way in or out of this place not covered by guards."

Nola stumbled, but Jeremy didn't notice.

There is a way out.

It had been pouring outside the domes that night. Dark sheets of rain that roared as they struck the glass. Nola's mother had gone to a conference at the domes on the far western side of the country. Dr. Wynne had been charged with watching Nola. Not that she needed it. She was fourteen. But it meant more time with Kieran. And Dr. Wynne had been too distracted to pay Nola or Kieran much mind anyway.

His research had been keeping him in the lab until all hours. His face had been growing paler and thinner for months.

"There has to be a way," he would mutter over and over as he wandered through the house. Kieran cleaned and made supper as he had done since his mother died. But there was something more to Dr. Wynne's ramblings now. More than his brilliance-bordering-on-madness, more than missing his wife. He had a secret.

Nola had spent many nights lying out on the roof of her house. She liked it up there. If she squinted, she could pretend there was no glass between her and the stars. More than once, she had seen a shadow coming out of the Wynne's house and disappearing into the night.

The last night Nola was to stay at the Wynne's, there had been a riot in the city. Nola had curled up on the couch, covering her ears, trying to block out the sounds that were too far away for her to hear. She watched as fire sprang up around the city. Flames danced on the glass. A fire so large, even the pounding rain couldn't douse it. The flames sent shadows swaying in the orange glow of the burning city.

"There won't be anything left if they keep burning sections of the city down," Kieran had said. "Don't they know they're destroying their own homes? Once the city is gone where will they live? Build huts and tents?"

"The rain will burn them like the fire," Nola had muttered, burying her face on Kieran's shoulder.

"Not tonight. The rain won't burn tonight. The clouds were white. There are still good days to bring hope. But they're hungry," Dr. Wynne spoke softly, the red glow of the city reflecting in his eyes, giving him the look of the mad scientist he had always threatened to become. "The rain didn't come this year.

And the clean water that fell wasn't enough to feed the plants. If you were starving, if you were watching your child starve, your anger would outweigh your reason. Their homes have been on fire for years. Only tonight, we can see the flames."

Tears streamed down Nola's cheeks. There were guards out there trying to protect the city dwellers, but the outsiders wouldn't see that. They would only see attack... never help.

"It's okay, Nola." Kieran wiped the tears from her face with his sleeve. "We're safe here." He laced his fingers through hers. "There are guards at every entrance and exit. No one could get in here without the guards stopping them."

"No," Dr. Wynne snapped, lifting his son by the collar.

Kieran staggered, his eyes wide with shock.

"There is no such thing as safe when the world is descending into madness. When the people burn the city, the palace will fall, too." Dr. Wynne clung desperately to his son. "One day, the outsiders will have had enough, and they will find a way into our paradise."

"But we can't have them all here," Nola said. "We don't have the resources."

"They will not come to join us." Dr. Wynne grasped Nola's shoulders, forcing her to look into his face. "They will come to destroy us. You have to know the way out."

Dr. Wynne grabbed Kieran and Nola by the hands and ran from the house, dragging them both behind him. He ran down the stone walkway and under the great willow tree. When they were nearing the far corner of the dome, he pulled them onto the grass and into a stand of trees.

Nola wanted to shout at him to stop, to scream they were safe. But something in the doctor's madness swept through her, and she followed, running as quickly as her feet could carry her. Dr. Wynne stopped inches before hitting the glass of the dome. They stood, staring into the darkness for a moment. Watching the rain stream down the outside. Nola pressed her face to the glass, looking to the west, where the fire was slowly beginning to die.

"When the time comes, and the only chance for survival is to go into the dying world, you must take the only way out," Dr. Wynne murmured.

Terror filled Kieran's eyes as his father knelt in front of the glass. Slowly, Dr. Wynne dug his fingers into the top corner of the bottom pane. With the tiniest scraping noise, the pane inched forward enough for him to squeeze his fingers in, pushing the panel to the side. The second layer of glass was still there, blocking them from the rain, but Dr. Wynne didn't hesitate. Pulling a penknife from his pocket, he shoved the blade into the crack where the pane met the metal beam, and the glass fell silently into his waiting hands.

"This is the way to salvation." The gleam of victory dancing in Dr. Wynne's eyes frightened Nola more than fires and riots.

Dr. Wynne crawled out of the passage he had created and into the rain. Spreading his arms wide, he gazed up into the storm. Lightning split the sky, silhouetting the triumphant form of Dr. Wynne.

Nola hadn't spoken to anyone about that night or the way out through the glass. Not even to Jeremy. Not even when the guards couldn't figure out how Dr. Wynne had been smuggling food to the city.

This is the way to salvation. And the way to Kieran.

CHAPTER SIX

Nola sat alone at the kitchen table, poking at the food on her plate and trying to do her reading for school.

The medicinal applications of plants must be weighed equally with their nutritional value. Also included in the assessment must be other species that would be required to maintain a proper habitat, and their accessibility—

There was a tap on the kitchen door.

"Coming," Nola called. Her heart dropped when she saw a giant shadow through the window.

Captain Ridgeway stood outside her door, his face somber.

"What happened to my mom?" Nola asked before Captain Ridgeway could speak. "Is she sick? Did she get hurt?"

Green Leaf is too far away. I don't know how to get to her.

"You're mother's fine." Captain Ridgeway stepped into the kitchen. As tall as Jeremy, Captain Ridgeway's well-muscled frame overwhelmed the tiny kitchen, leaving Nola no room to breathe.

"Oh." Nola clasped her shaking hands together. "What happened? Is somebody dead? Is Jeremy okay?"

"There was an incident in the city last night," Captain Ridgeway said. "There was a fight between two groups that accelerated to the point where the Outer Guard had to become involved."

"But everyone's all right?"

"There were a few injuries," Captain Ridgeway's voice dropped.

"Gentry?" Nola knew she was right before Captain Ridgeway nodded.

He's not just an Outer Guard. He's Jeremy and Gentry's father.

"Is she going to be all right?" Nola pictured Gentry, tall and strong with short, blond hair framing her round face. Always laughing, but now she was hurt.

"She'll recover," Captain Ridgeway said. "But there were a few deaths. The packs that were attacking each other dragged in bystanders that shouldn't have been involved in their fight."

"Werewolves," Nola breathed.

"Nothing travels faster than rumors in the domes," Captain Ridgeway said without surprise. "When we searched the casualties for identification, we found dome medicine on one of the deceased."

The room swayed.

"You lost your I-Vent?" Captain Ridgeway continued.

Nola nodded, not trusting her voice.

"Is there anyone who stood out to you at the Charity Center? Anyone who tried to get close to you?"

Nola shook her head.

"If someone is stealing dome medicine, we need to know," Captain Ridgeway said, his eyes searching Nola's face.

"I just lost my I-Vent," Nola said, her voice shaking. "I think I..."

Kieran dead. Killed by werewolves.

"I dropped it. The person who had the medicine—"

"Is dead. But that doesn't mean there isn't someone out there trying to steal dome supplies. If a black market for our medicine is creeping into the city, it needs to be stopped immediately. Did you see anything suspicious? Anything at all?"

"I don't know," Nola said.

Captain Ridgeway nodded, his eyes still locked on Nola's face. "If you remember anything, please come to me immediately."

"But—" Nola stepped in front of the Captain as he turned toward the door. "No one we know, none of our people died?"

"No. All the guards will recover."

He stepped outside and shut the door behind him with a sharp *click*.

Nola slid down the wall, her head in her hands.

All the guards will recover.

But what about Kieran?

Had he been trapped between the wolf packs?

What if someone had stolen the I-Vent from him? What if he had lied, and he was the one who needed the medicine? What if he was the one they had found the medicine on?

He could be dying. He could be dead, and she would never know.

Nola pressed her palms together, trying to stop her hands from shaking. Her breath came in panicked gasps.

Kieran torn apart by wolves.

I have to know.

Nola sprang to her feet, willing herself to move quickly enough she wouldn't have time to change her mind.

There was only one way to know if Kieran was alive.

5th and Nightland.

CHAPTER SEVEN

The damp chill of the night air cut through Nola's coat. The wind had pushed the stench of the city all the way up to the domes. Nola crouched just outside the glass, like a child reaching for something dangerous with the certainty someone would snatch it away before she could get hurt.

A night bird soared overhead, cawing at the darkness. Nola jumped at the sound, flattening herself against the glass. The bird kept flying into the distance, not caring that Nola stood alone in the dark. She waited for a moment, counting each breath of outside air. She pulled out her I-Vent and took a deep breath of the medicine. But still, no guards came charging toward her.

I'm alone.

Carefully, she knelt and slid the outer glass so it was nearly in place. No one passing would see anything amiss, but there was enough space to squeeze her fingers in to push the pane aside.

She stood and turned toward the city. Lights glowed through the haze that hung over the buildings. She wanted to turn and crawl back into the dome and into her warm bed where she could pretend Captain Ridgeway had never come to the kitchen door.

Kieran.

She took a step forward. And then another. She would do this. She would find Kieran.

One road ran from the domes to the city. The only path with lights and guards. Nola stayed away from the road, cutting through the old forest.

She had seen pictures of what the forest had looked like before, when her mother had been young and the founders were still building the domes. The trees here had been thick and lush, their branches so dense the sunlight could barely peek through to the forest floor.

But the trees had begun to die a long time ago. A few still had leaves clinging to them. Most now stood like skeletons—dead and barren.

The moon peered through the clouds, and the naked branches cast strange shadows onto the ground.

Keep moving, Nola. Just keep moving.

One foot, then the other. A single step at a time. Moving deeper into the woods.

Did animals still live in these trees? Or worse, had people too poor to live in the slums of the city dared to make the dead forest their home?

Nola moved as quickly and quietly as she could. Every now and then, a rustle in the distance would send her sprinting for a few minutes, fleeing from the unseen danger.

Soon she neared the edge of the woods, and the city rose above her. She cut to the left toward the bridge that led into the city. The river roared beneath her. The foul stench of chemicals and rot sent bile into her throat. How many times had the bus taken them to the city, and she had never smelled the river like this. She had always been sheltered from the worst of it by the technology of the domes.

Shadows stalked across the bridge. Some in groups, some alone. Nola clenched her fists in her pockets, wishing she had thought to grab a heavy stick or rock from the woods. Anything to defend herself with.

She quickened her pace, trying not to walk so fast as to seem scared. The metal of the bridge gave a dull *thunk* every time she took a step. Nola kept her eyes forward, moving with purpose, pretending she belonged.

She was halfway over the bridge and could see the streets in front of her. The Outer Guard patrolled the city at night. If she had to call for help, would she be banished from the domes?

A group of people near Nola's age had bunched together at the city end of the bridge. Talking and laughing like the reek of the river and danger of the night meant nothing. Both the boys and girls wore torn up leather clothes. The girls' tops were ripped in deep Vs, letting their pale skin gleam in the night as they hung from the boys' arms. The pairs all stood under one man, bigger and older than the rest. He perched on the railing of the bridge, holding court over those beneath him.

Nola turned her gaze away from the group. She was almost off the bridge. She could see the seam where metal met concrete.

The man who stood on the railing turned to look at her. His cheeks sunk into his pale face, a scruffy beard covered his chin, and in the glow of the city lights, the man's eyes gleamed a deep, blood red. He smiled, and a sound like a wolf growling rumbled from his throat before he tipped his head to the sky. Flinging his arms to his sides, the man howled. The group around him threw their heads back, joining him.

Nola ran, not knowing if they would follow or where she was going. Her feet pounded on the concrete as the howling rent the night.

Werewolves.

Jeremy hadn't been lying. Lycan changed people. Wolves filled the city.

She turned a corner and pressed herself into the shadows of a building.

5th and Nightland. Just get to 5th and Nightland.

A sign on the corner that appeared to have been painted over and over again read *12th Street*, the other read *Rotland* in an untidy scrawl. Nola's hands trembled. She closed her eyes, picturing the maps of the city in her mind. The number was right, but the name was wrong. Who had renamed the streets of the city, and why had she never known?

North. Go north to find 5th.

Staying close to the buildings in the depths of the shadows, Nola walked, keeping her head down, trying to picture what the city would have looked like when it was still prosperous. When the river water was clean, and people rode in boats on its glittering surface.

11th Street. 10th.

What would it have been like to live in a city in the open air, with parks to play in and a whole world to explore?

Nola passed a dark stairway leading down to a basement.

A hand reached out, grabbing her leg.

"Please," a woman's voice came from the shadows, low and crackling. "Please, do you have any change?"

"No." Nola stumbled back, wrenching her leg from the woman's weak grasp. "I don't have any money."

It was true. They didn't use money in the domes. Currency had always been a vague concept—numbers on a screen, not something to be kept in a pocket.

"You're strong," the woman muttered, crawling up the stairs. "Vamp. Do you have Vamp?" The woman dragged herself into the light of the street lamps. Wrinkles covered her thin face. Cracks split her dried lips, and the skin under her eyes hung loose in horrible bags. "I'm dying!" the woman shrieked, trying to push herself up but crumpling to the ground. "You have Vamp. I know you do!"

"I don't." Nola shook her head, backing away from the woman. "I'm sorry. I can't help you."

"Lycan, ReVamp. Please!" the woman screamed after her as Nola ran down the street. "I'm dying. Murderer!"

Nola ran from the woman, not caring who saw her, her only thought to escape from the echo of the woman's voice.

Murderer!

In her haze of panic, she almost ran right past the sign that read *5th Street* and *Blood Way*.

Turning her back to the river, Nola walked west down 5th. There were lights in the windows here. And the farther she walked, the more people there were on the streets, some walking on the cracked pavement, some sitting in doorways. The scent of the river had disappeared, replaced by the stale smell of humans and animals living too close together.

The back of Nola's neck prickled with the feeling of a dozen people staring at her back.

"You," a voice called from behind her.

Nola quickened her pace.

"Don't bother trying to get away," the voice said. A moment later a hand had locked around her arm.

Nola clenched her fists, ready to punch whomever had grabbed her, but the man already had her by both wrists.

"Please, I don't have—" Nola began.

"Anything but a dome jacket?" the man said, eyebrows raised.

Nola glanced down at her coat. It was plain black, made for warmth, not protection from the sun or acid rain. But the man's coat was tattered and dirty, like everything else in the city. Nola's looked brand new.

"Why would a Domer be out on the streets this late at night?" the man asked, tightening his ice-cold grip on her wrists. "A little thing like you clearly isn't an Outer Guard."

"I'm looking for someone." Nola tipped her chin up, staring into the man's eyes.

His irises were black, leaving voids where color should have been.

"Who?"

"That's none of your business," Nola said, trying to sound confident the man wasn't going to kill her in the middle of the street.

"Look, sweetheart," the man whispered in her ear. His breath smelled of iron as it wafted over her. "I don't care if you're here to buy Vamp or get laid. But this is my territory. If a Domer gets killed here, we'll have the Outer Guard after our heads, and the last thing I want is a riot getting all my people killed. Believe it or not, I'm probably the only thing standing between you and getting your throat ripped open."

Nola gasped as the man squeezed her wrists so tight she thought they might break.

"Tell me who you want to see so I can make you somebody else's problem to clean up."

"Kieran," Nola said, "Kieran Wynne. I'm supposed to be able to find him at 5th and Nightland."

The man cursed under his breath. "I love it when the hero sends a pretty girl to die."

"He's my friend."

The man took her by the shoulders, steering her roughly down the street.

"Friends don't send friends into Vamp territory," the man said.

Fear shot through Nola's body, setting fire to every nerve.

"What, sweetheart?" the man hissed. "You didn't know you were being saved by a monster?"

He smiled, showing two long fangs in the front of his mouth.

Nola swallowed her scream.

The man gripped her tighter, shoving her down the street. "The better to eat you with, my dear."

"That's the wolf's line," Nola said. A Vamper was steering her through the dark. What would people think when she wasn't in the domes tomorrow? How long would it be before they noticed?

They'll never find me.

"Be glad a wolf didn't grab you," the Vamper laughed. "They like to fight and die. And if you think all this shit with vampires and werewolves is going to work out like a fairytale, this really is your first time in the city. Here"—the Vamper pushed her up onto the curb—"5th and Nightland. Have your friend get you out, if you make it that long. The next time you cross through my territory, I'll let them have you. They'll dump your dried up body into the river before the Domers know you're gone."

The man turned and strode away, leaving Nola alone under a flickering street lamp.

She looked up at the sign. 5th Street and Nightland. But there was no one in sight. No one waiting to give her help, no sign reading *find Kieran alive and healthy here.*

Where are you, Kieran?

Nola closed her eyes. A very small, very foolish part of her thought when she opened her eyes Kieran would be there. Or maybe if she called his name he would appear.

When she opened her eyes, there was nothing in front of her but an empty street. Maybe the Outer Guard had raided the area? Why would they need to raid a place where Kieran would be?

Muffled voices came from nearby, but Nola couldn't see anyone. No lights on in the houses, no people roaming the streets.

A thumping pounded from below her feet. A strong, steady rhythm. Like music. Nola studied the ground. Trash, dirt, and soot covered the cracked sidewalk.

Something white twenty feet away caught her eye. The thumping grew louder as she approached. Voices became distinct, and a melody broke through the noise. A metal trapdoor had been built into the sidewalk, a single word painted across its surface. *Nightland.*

Nola reached into the hole in the metal door just big enough for a hand and tried to lift. She gritted her teeth against the weight of the metal, but the door didn't budge.

She took a breath and tried again, pulling until pain shot

through her shoulders. Panting, she let go of the door and staggered back a step.

Go to Nightland, find Kieran. I have to find Kieran.

"I have come too far to get turned back by a door."

Taking a deep breath, she stomped three times on the metal. The sound echoed through the empty street, and the noise from below changed.

The music still thumped on, but the voices were different. Their tones loud and urgent.

Nola jumped back as the metal door flew open with a *clang* that shook her ears. Four people leapt onto the sidewalk.

Each of them held a weapon in their hand—a pipe, a sword, a staff, and a knife. The four glared at Nola. She took another step back, missed the curb and fell into the street.

A woman with bright purple and scarlet-streaked hair stood over Nola, twirling a knife in her hand.

"Such a pretty little thing to be knocking on our door." The woman grinned.

A dark-skinned man with scars dotting his face stepped up next to her, digging his staff into the pavement beside Nola's neck. "Did someone order dinner?" The man had fangs, like the one who had brought her here.

"Bring her inside," the man with the sword said.

"Not worth the risk," the man with the pipe said, staring at Nola with frightening hunger.

"Then we kill her out here." The woman raised her knife.

"Kieran!" Nola shouted, covering her face, waiting for the blade to strike. Even if he heard her scream she would already be dead.

"What did you say?" the woman said.

"Kieran," Nola said, uncovering her face. "I'm here to see Kieran Wynne."

"How do you know Kieran?" The woman lifted Nola to her feet by the collar of her coat.

"F-from the domes," Nola stammered.

"But how did you find out about Nightland?" The man with the pipe sneered, showing his frighteningly white teeth.

"He told me," Nola said.

The woman lifted her higher so her toes barely reached the ground.

"He came to the Charity Center. He stole my I-Vent and left a note in my pocket. It said to find him at 5th and Nightland."

The woman let go of Nola's collar, and she fell back onto the pavement, cracking her head against the stone.

"You're the one." The man with the staff tilted his head from side to side as he stared at Nola. "If the boy wants her..." He shrugged.

"Is Kieran alive?" Nola asked as the man with the sword lifted her to her feet and clamped a hand firmly around her arm.

"If you don't mind"—the man ignored Nola's question. His tone and accent sounded strange, like he wasn't from the city—"I would suggest you not try and run away. I'm sure it was quite a feat for you to make it here from the domes alone, but I promise, if you go off on your own, you won't survive Nightland."

The man with the staff struck the metal door four times, pausing for a moment before repeating the four beats. The sound echoed through the streets. The Outer Guard would hear.

They'll save me.

The door swung open, and the pounding rhythm of the music drifted up into the night. Kieran could be down there. Nola didn't know if she wanted to be rescued by the Outer Guard or not.

The man with the sword bowed, still keeping a grip on Nola's arm as he gestured down the steps. "Welcome to Nightland."

CHAPTER EIGHT

The metal stairs vibrated under Nola's feet, but the music ate the sound of her steps.

The woman with the scarlet and purple hair waited at the bottom, knife still drawn. Once all of them had descended below the street, two men appeared from the shadows and closed the door. It was thicker than Nola had realized. At least three inches of heavy metal, as thick as the doors to the outside in the atrium. But the two men lowered it back into place as if the weight were nothing and bolted the door shut.

Nola's heart raced.

There's no way out. I'm trapped underground.

Even if there weren't guards, she would never be able to lift that door.

"If you please," the sword man said, sliding his blade back into the sheath at his waist. The sword looked new, and its embossed leather sheath shone with fresh black polish.

Who makes new swords and sheaths?

The woman walked in front, leading them down another set of stairs. The music grew louder with each step, and flashing lights bounced across the landing below.

Nola's gasp was lost in the music as the room came into view. Hundreds of people in a seething mass, all moving to the same rhythm. Arches were carved into the walls of the room, some leading nowhere, some disappearing into darkness. The smell of sweat, metal, and dust permeated the air. It was different from the stench of the city. A scent as primal as the dancers, all swaying to the music, some alone, some wound tightly around their partners.

The woman walked into the crowd, and the dancers parted, leaving a path as though frightened of the woman. A few of them stared at Nola, speaking loudly to their fellows, but Nola could only make out one word over the music: *Domer.*

They drew near to the speakers, and the sound vibrated in Nola's chest, sending her heart sprinting. She balled her fists tightly, letting her nails bite into her skin, willing herself not to panic. She could hear now that there were words in the music, but she couldn't tell what they said.

The woman turned left, heading toward an arch that was blocked off by another heavy metal door.

A woman as tall as any man Nola had ever met stood beside the door, her arms crossed and her face set in a grimace. She nodded at the woman with the knife and opened the door. The scraping of the metal against the concrete floor cut through the music, slicing into Nola's ears.

As soon as they entered the dark passage, the door screeched shut behind them, dampening the music. Nola glanced back. Only the four who had been aboveground accompanied her now.

The woman led on, and the man with the sword didn't let go of her arm. Dim lights were set into the ceiling of the tunnel, leaving shadows for them to pass through every few steps.

"What is this place?" Nola asked, half-choking on the damp smell of the tunnel, panic squeezing her chest.

We're twenty feet underground. Maybe thirty. Far enough for the weight of the earth to crush us.

"Nightland," the woman said.

They walked in silence for a moment. The pounding of the music faded, and the walls muffled the sounds of their footsteps.

The ceiling here was short, barely above the sword man's head. The woman at the door to the tunnel would have needed to hunch to walk down it.

The walls swayed, closing in around them. Smothering Nola in dirt.

Nola blinked, willing the walls to hold still.

"You all right?" the sword man asked, raising a sculpted black eyebrow at Nola.

"She's fine," the man with the pipe said. "She's from the domes. If the air bothers her, she can just use her I-Vent."

"Not the air," Nola said. Her voice sounded faint even to her own ears. She took a deep breath and tried to sound stronger. "I don't like being underground."

The woman with the knife laughed, her voice bouncing down the tunnel. "And Kieran asked you to come here? And I thought you must be an old friend of his."

"I am," Nola said. "What is this place?"

"Nightla—"

"What is Nightland?" Nola cut the woman off.

It was the man with the staff's turn to laugh. "Nightland is exactly what it sounds like, Domer. It's the land of the night dwellers, and you just wandered into it."

Night dwellers. Impossibly heavy doors. People in the city who roamed the night. All of those people were dancing, not coughing, not sick. Dancing underground in the night.

Vampers. Kieran led me to a Vamper den.

Nola stopped walking and almost toppled over as the man continued. But his grip on her arm was so strong she couldn't fall to the floor. He held her up without seeming to notice.

She should run away or shout for help. But there was nowhere to go and no one to hear.

"What are your names?" Nola swallowed hard. "I'm Magnolia." Maybe if they thought of her as human, like them, not as a meal. But were they human? If a drug changed you that much....

"Raina," the woman said, looking back at Nola. The turning of her head sent her purple and scarlet hair dancing in the dim light.

"That's Julian."

The man with the sword and the dark shining hair bowed his head. "It's a pleasure."

"Desmond."

The dark-skinned man with hundreds of tiny scars gave a jerk of his head.

"And Bryant."

The man with the pipe didn't acknowledge Nola.

"Those are great names," Nola said.

"What were you expecting?" Desmond asked, his voice a low grumble.

"Something along the lines of Fang, Shade, Bloodlust, and Satan I expect," Julian said.

"I-I meant," Nola stammered, hoping accidentally being rude wasn't enough of a reason to eat a person, "that it is lovely to meet all of you. And thank you for bringing me safely to Kieran."

"Don't worry, Domer," Bryant said from behind. "We won't hurt you. Not before you get to see Kieran."

"So, he's alive?" Nola's heart leapt into her throat. "Kieran's fine?"

"I don't think our definitions of *fine* would match." Raina sneered, baring her teeth.

Nola tensed. Kieran was alive. He would protect her. Kieran wouldn't let them drink her blood. He had told her to come here.

He wouldn't lead me here to watch me die.

They walked in silence. Every once in a while, there would be a metal door in the wall, or another tunnel twisting away into the darkness.

Nola tried to remember each time they turned. But there were no arrows on the walls like in the domes. No signs pointing the way. And even if she could remember the path, there was no way she could get back the way she came. Not unless they wanted her to go.

"How big is this place?" Nola asked, more to break the endless pounding of their footfalls than because she actually wanted to know.

"No idea," Raina said. "I don't own a measuring tape."

"Then how much longer until we get there?" Nola asked. She didn't know how long it had taken her to find Nightland or how long she had been down here.

If I'm not back in the domes by sunrise . . .

"We'll be there soon," Julian said as the tunnel began to widen and slope downward.

"Where is *there*?" Nola's voice shook. How far underground were they now?

The tunnel widened even more, and the doors along the walls became more frequent. Soon they were passing people in the hall. Some nodded, others averted their eyes, but all of them gave the group a wide berth.

Brick and stone replaced the dirt of the walls. The lights were evenly spaced, giving the hall a more populated feel. The doors were still made of metal, but they didn't look as though they were meant to withstand a bomb blast.

Two boys a few years younger than Nola ran down the hall, laughing, only falling silent as they passed the group. Nola could hear their laughter begin again behind her.

A sudden jerk shot pain through Nola's arm. Raina had stopped in front of an antique-looking, intricately carved wooden door, and Julian held Nola in place.

Raina knocked, and the sound echoed through the hall. Shadows passed behind a small piece of glass set in the door.

Slowly, the door opened. Nola had hoped Kieran would come running through and tell Julian to let go of her arm where she could feel bruises forming. But instead, a tall man whom she had never seen before stood in front of her, his arms crossed as he stared at the group. Young and handsome, he had curling black hair down to his shoulders. His skin looked as though it should have been a deep olive but had grown pale without the sun. And the man's eyes were dark with black irises the same as the man who had led her to Nightland.

Nola glanced at Julian. His eyes were black as well.

"Emanuel." Raina bowed. "This Domer showed up at the gate. She said Kieran Wynne told her to find him here."

Emanuel examined Nola, starting from her feet and ending with her brown hair. "She looks like the right one. Nola?"

"Yes." Nola nodded. "How do you know my name?"

"Kieran told me about the girl who gives Eden breath." Emanuel smiled. "I'm glad you decided to brave the outside world. Bring her." Emanuel turned and walked away.

Julian steered Nola through the door, and Bryant closed it behind them. The inside of the door had been built of the same heavy metal as the door that led to the street. The intricate wood was only a façade.

Nola turned to Emanuel but gasped at the space around her. They were in a chamber larger than Nola's whole house. But instead of bare walls, beautiful art decorated this room.

Paintings, like the ones Nola had only ever seen on computer screens, adorned the tops of the walls. In the center of the ceiling hung three large crystal chandeliers, bathing all the paintings in their warm light. In one corner sat a piano and in another a harp. Below the paintings, the walls were covered with bookshelves, six feet tall and packed with books.

"Wow," Nola whispered.

"It's beautiful, isn't it?" Emanuel said. "These things would have been destroyed aboveground. Burned in the riots or for warmth, but we decided to protect them. You see, the Domers care about protecting the genetics of the human race. But down here, we want to protect what it is to be human. Sometimes, things have to change in order to survive. It all depends on which part of ourselves we're willing to give up. Some choose the body, others choose the soul."

Nola's mind raced, trying to take in everything in the room and understand what Emanuel was saying at the same time. She wanted to ask them to stop and let her look at the paintings or touch just one of the books, but they led her on and out through the far side of the room. They entered what appeared to be a home. Dark and, Nola shivered, underground, but a house nonetheless.

An older woman hovered over a stove, and a little girl clung to her skirt. She reached up to Emanuel as they walked by, but he shook his head at the child and kept walking. Hurt filled the little girl's big brown eyes as the group moved past the kitchen. Open doors to rooms filled with beds came next and then a steel door. Emanuel pushed the door open, and they all stepped through.

CHAPTER NINE

Nola caught a flash of scrubbed metal tables and brick walls draped in clear plastic before a voice shouted "Nola!" and Kieran's arms were around her.

"You're not dead," Nola breathed, burying her face in Kieran's jacket. "I thought you were dead."

"I'm fine," Kieran whispered. "I told you the medicine wasn't for me."

"But Captain Ridgeway found dome medicine on a dead body. After a riot." Tears streamed down Nola's face. "I thought it was you. I had to see if you were alright."

"I'm fine." Kieran pressed his lips to her forehead. "I'm fine. And you're safe here."

"Safe?" Nola half-shrieked. "There was a werewolf pack on the bridge. A sick woman was begging me for help, and I didn't have anything to give her. And then a Vamper almost killed me. He dragged me out of his territory and told me not to come back. I don't know how I'm going to get home, if I even have time before they find out I'm gone and decide they don't want me in the domes anymore."

"Are all Domer girls this hysterical?" Raina asked from her place by the door.

"Oh, no." Dr. Wynne appeared behind his son's shoulder. His hair stuck out at strange angles and had turned almost completely gray now, and his skin was nearly translucent in its pallor. "Nola is usually quite calm and reasonable. She is simply not used to our element, so you'll just have to be patient while she adjusts." He gave Nola a fatherly pat on the shoulder, muttering, "It is good to see you," before wandering back to his worktable.

"If it's good to see me"—Nola rounded on Kieran—"then why didn't you warn me what was at 5th and Nightland?"

"No one asked you to come here," Raina said. "I certainly didn't ask for a Domer to ruin my night."

"Raina," Emanuel said, silencing her. "How could we have known if you would turn us in?" Emanuel stared intently into Nola's eyes.

"Or that you weren't dumb enough to get yourself killed your first trip outside the domes." Raina shrugged as Emanuel turned his gaze to her.

"I'll make sure you get home before dawn." Kieran took Nola's hand. "I won't let them find out you're here. I won't let them banish you."

"I thought you were dead," Nola said to Kieran, keeping her voice low though she knew the rest of the room could hear. "You stole my I-Vent, left me a note telling me how to find you, and now I'm in a den full of Vampers."

"We prefer the proper name: *vampire*. Vamper is a rather nasty term. Rather like us calling you Domer. But I should give you some credit. At least you're smart enough to have figured that part out," Julian said in a genial tone. "Although Desmond's fangs do rather give it away."

"Kieran, why are you here?" Nola gripped Kieran's hand, hanging onto the one thing in the room that didn't terrify her.

"I think it's time we had a talk," Emanuel said, gesturing for Nola to sit at the large metal table.

The table looked like a slab for a corpse, not a place to sit for a pleasant chat.

"Emanuel—" Kieran began, but Emanuel silenced him with the wave of a hand.

"It is providence that you traveled to us tonight." Emanuel pointed again for Nola to sit.

Nola nodded and took a seat at the table. Kieran sat next to her, his smile disappearing as his brow furrowed.

"Raina, if you could—" Emanuel started.

"Get the Domer some refreshments?" Raina said, her tone barely polite. "Of course. The woman will go to the kitchen and get some snacks for the guest." She spun and walked out of the room.

Julian shut the door, leaving Bryant and Desmond standing on either side like guards, neither putting away his weapon.

"I must admit, Nola," Emanuel said, "we did have a courier that was caught up in the unfortunate incident last night. And he had an item with him. Something we need very badly. Where do we begin?" Emanuel took a seat across the shining metal table.

"With Fletcher," Dr. Wynne said. "If you want her to understand, you have to start with Fletcher."

Emanuel sat for a long moment. "Before you were born, before even Dr. Wynne was born, the Incorporation started building the domes. Forty-two sites around the world. To be filled with the best and the brightest. Not only to encourage research, but also to protect the gene pool. People were sick, dying. Cancer had become a plague. Clean water was scarce, and food supplies were in danger. But that wasn't what the people who created the domes feared.

"Fertility rates were dropping, and birth defects were becoming more common. The Incorporation had to protect the future of the human race by making sure it could breed.

That's what the signs read, what was spouted at every conference. *To protect our children.*" Emanuel spat the last sentence. "But soon, the people realized it wasn't all the children the Incorporation were trying to protect, just the chosen few who lived in the domes. The rest of the population was left out here to watch their children suffer and die. The sicknesses became worse. But all of the researchers were in the domes. The brilliant minds were gone, and we were left with Fletcher."

"I've never heard of a researcher named Fletcher," Nola said.

"You wouldn't have," Kieran said. "They don't talk about him in the domes."

"People were in pain, and Fletcher came up with a new medicine. A drug that could stop tumors from growing. Make lungs impervious to the filth in the air. The medicine made people strong and slowed the natural aging process."

"That's amazing," Nola said.

"But the cure came at a price. Sensitivity to light. The inability to metabolize normal food, the reliance on blood for nutrition. Anger, violence, bloodlust. It changed you to the very core. But it was a way to survive. At first, the drug was only given to a few people. The ones who were very ill, on the brink of death. But soon, others outside Fletcher's control began to manufacture the drug, and it spread like wildfire."

"Vamp," Nola said, studying Emanuel's black eyes. "Vamp was made to be a medicine?"

"Not all vampires set out with the intent to wander the night. We were trying to survive. Vampires are what we had to become. There was no other choice," Emanuel said.

"But the wolves," Nola began.

"Someone tried to improve Vamp. To alter the way Vamp affects the ability to eat food."

"So, it is true." Nola swallowed the burning in her throat. "Vampires drink blood."

"Animal blood," Kieran said, reaching for Nola and pulling his hand away when she flinched.

"Nightland does not allow vampires who hunt for human blood," Emanuel said.

"But there are some who do?" Nola asked.

"You met one tonight," Julian said. "The man who showed you here, he was from a group who drink from humans. Almost all those who live aboveground do."

"Wolves are able to eat but suffer pheromone changes that alter the way they interact with each other," Emanuel said.

"Packs," Nola said. "It makes them run in packs."

"Yes," Kieran said, "which makes them more dangerous than any of the vampires."

"Ours is the only real community of vampires," Emanuel said. "Most prefer to roam and hunt on their own. There are turf lords, and territorial groups, but they would kill each other without hesitation for fresh blood. We have banded together in Nightland because we want something more. More than injecting Vamp and living to breathe another night. We want a chance for the children on the outside."

"And that is where I come in." Dr. Wynne spun his chair around and faced the group as though he had been waiting for his cue. "Vamp has a tendency to alter the user's moods. With the increase in strength comes increased aggression. With the need to drink blood comes a taste for violence."

"And the eyes, and the teeth," Nola said, her gaze darting to Emanuel's eyes.

"The eyes, yes," Emanuel said.

"The teeth are prosthetic," Desmond said from behind Nola. "If I'm going to be called a vampire, I might as well embrace it. Besides, it makes hunting easier."

"Desmond," Dr. Wynne said, flapping his hands as though fangs were trivial, "lived as a roamer for a long time and has no personal aversion to human blood." He paused, scratching his head for a moment. "But if there were a way to create a new formula of Vamp, one that would make people strong and healthy without subjecting them to the unfortunate side effects, we would have essentially found a cure. A way for people to live healthily on the outside without constant fear of contamination and death."

"That's what he's working on. ReVamp," Kieran said. "It would keep people healthy and keep the streets safe."

Nola ran through it in her mind. The woman who had begged her for help. The little boys at the Charity Center. All healthy.

"You could save everyone," she breathed.

"Not everyone," Emanuel said softly before looking to Desmond. "Fetch Eden."

"What's Eden?" Nola asked.

"Eden isn't a what," Emanuel said. "Eden is a who."

Emanuel nodded, and Desmond opened the door, disappearing into the hall.

"Before you meet her, I want to thank you," Emanuel said. "Without you, we would have lost her already."

Desmond returned, holding the small girl from the kitchen in his arms. As soon as the little girl's big brown eyes found Emanuel, she reached out, wanting him to hold her. Emanuel stood and took the child, kissing her gently on the cheek before kneeling next to Nola.

"This is Eden," Emanuel said. Eden hid her face on his chest. "She is my child."

"She's beautiful," Nola said.

"Eden," Emanuel said. The little girl turned her eyes back to her father. "Can you say thank you? This is the nice girl who gave you your medicine."

"Thank you," Eden said so softly her words could barely be heard.

"Good girl." Emanuel kissed her black curls that matched his own.

He handed Eden to Desmond, who slipped back out of the room.

"That's why I stole your I-Vent," Kieran whispered. "She needs the medicine."

"Eden has tumors in her lungs," Emanuel said. "They were getting bad enough she couldn't breathe. Your I-Vent bought her more time."

More time for a little girl with big brown eyes. Someone so small shouldn't be so sick.

"I'm so sorry. An I-Vent can't cure tumors," Nola said. "But when Dr. Wynne finishes ReVamp, he can cure her."

"Vamp, Lycan, ReVamp"—Emanuel gripped the table. The shining metal bent under his grasp—"they all have consequences."

"You just said—"

"If you're too sick or too young," Julian said, "all of the drugs can kill you. Or worse."

"What's worse?" Nola's heart raced as though she already knew the answer.

"Zombies." Julian glanced at Emanuel. "If the body rejects the drug, the body will start to decay. Beginning with the mind. All that's left is a craving for human flesh. Zombies would eat their own family without a thought. They know no pain. No fear. Only hunger. You've probably never seen such a thing."

"I have," Nola said, swallowing the bile that once again rose in her throat. "The zombies come to the domes sometimes. The guards drug them and take them away for treatment."

"There is no treatment," Emanuel said, his voice breaking. "There is no medicine that can cure a zombie. There is no medicine in the outside world that can save Eden."

"But there is in the domes." Dr. Wynne placed a hand on Nola's shoulder.

"I had a contact from far outside the city," Emanuel said. "He had managed to procure the medicine Eden needs."

"But he didn't make it all the way to Nightland," Kieran said.

"And somehow," Emanuel said, his black eyes studying Nola's face, "you did. And you have brought hope with you."

"We would only need a vial," Kieran said, "and that little girl could live until she's old enough—"

"To become a vampire," Nola said.

"To live to see twenty," Emanuel said. He reached across the table and took Nola's hand. His fingers were colder than the metal surface. "It's such a small thing in the world of the domes, but it's my daughter's life out here."

"You want me to steal medicine from the domes?" Nola pulled her hand out of Emanuel's reach.

"I am asking you as a father to save my daughter's life. I'm not asking as an outsider, or as a vampire. I am asking as a human, a man who is terrified. I am no different from you."

"You are." Nola stood up. "And not because I'm from the domes and you're an outsider. You are a vampire. You're asking me to help vampires."

"We are all humans." Julian spread his arms as though reaching out to every person in the city. "We've done what we had to in order to survive. But we are still humans. Can't you try to see us that way?"

"If you want to be seen as human, why would you name yourselves after monsters?" Nola asked. "Why would you choose to be called something so evil?"

"We've been forced to live in the dark for years. Is it so strange we would name ourselves after children of the night?" Raina asked as she pushed open the door, carrying a tray of tea. "We are living the nightmare. But we didn't choose it. We were abandoned out here. We're just the ones that have become strong enough to survive."

"Nola," Dr. Wynne said, "that little girl will be dead within the month. We need one vial. One tiny tube to save her. And you're the only one who can get it."

"But you know how to get into the domes." Nola shook her head. "You're the one who showed me how to get out."

"The medicine is in medical storage. You have to get to the lower levels to get near the room," Dr. Wynne said.

"And your mom works right down the hall from medical storage," Kieran said, his voice low and steady as he took Nola's hand in his. "All you have to do is visit her and then take a detour. No one will ever know."

"And if I get caught?" Nola said. "If they banish me for stealing from the domes?"

Forced to live in Nightland, stuck in a living tomb for the rest of my life.

"Tell them I broke in," Dr. Wynne said. "Tell them I came to your room and threatened to kill you if you didn't do it. They already believe me insane. I'm sure they can believe I could become violent."

"They would send the Outer Guard after you." Nola's mouth went dry in her panic.

"A worthy risk to save a child's life." Dr. Wynne shrugged and went back to his work.

"You won't get caught." Kieran took both of Nola's hands. "I know how you can do it. All you have to do is trust me. Please, Nola. For me."

Nola found herself nodding before she knew she had made a choice.

CHAPTER TEN

Nola clutched her hot tea, afraid her trembling hands would give away her fear if she lifted the cup to her mouth.

Dr. Wynne spoke first, explaining to Nola exactly what medicine he needed. Then Julian appeared, bringing with him maps of the domes.

"How did you get this?" Nola reached for the map. Bright Dome was there with her house drawn in the far corner.

"All the domes were built the same," Julian said, "and the Wynnes aren't the only ones who have left."

Nola's shoulders tensed at the word *left. Left* didn't seem to describe it.

"Under the circumstances, I would think you would be grateful for the breach in dome security as it will make your job that much easier. Medical storage is here." Julian pointed to a small square space. "It's environmentally controlled."

"Cold storage," Dr. Wynne said. "It'll be in the back cage."

"Isn't medical storage locked?" Nola asked.

"It is," Dr. Wynne said, "but seed storage isn't. And they share a vent system."

"All you have to do is go see your mom," Kieran said. "You're still planning on going the botany route?"

"It's not like I have a choice," Nola said.

"Head into seed storage," Kieran said. "No one will question why you're there. Go through the vent."

"Go through?" Nola pushed away from the table, her heart racing at the mere thought of entering such a small, dark place. "You want me to climb into a vent!"

"Only for a minute," Kieran said. "And then once you have the vial, you walk out the door and back to your room. I'll come into the domes tomorrow night and get the medicine from you." He took Nola's face in his hands. "You can do this, Nola."

"You shouldn't risk coming back into the domes," Nola said. "If they catch you..."

"They won't," Kieran said.

"When your mother returns from Green Leaf tomorrow," Emanuel said, "will she be going back to her lab?"

"She will." Nola nodded. "She'll go straight to the lab to check on her samples before she comes home. She'll make a guard bring her bag to our house. It's what she always does."

Kieran nodded to Emanuel.

"Then go see your mother as soon as you can," Emanuel said. "Eden is depending on you."

The room fell silent for a moment. Nola wanted to say something brave, or hopeful, but her mind buzzed with fatigue.

"Your walking into Nightland was providence, Nola," Emanuel said. "Even in the darkest of places, hope can appear."

"We should get you home," Kieran said, standing up and laying his hand on Nola's shoulder.

"I won't make it back before dawn," Nola said. "How long have I been down here?"

I should have brought a watch.

Kieran looked at Emanuel who nodded to Desmond and Bryant. Both men stepped aside, and Raina opened the door.

"There's a shortcut to the domes," Kieran said. "I'll take you."

"Raina, Julian," Emanuel said, "make sure Nola gets home safe."

Kieran's hand tensed on Nola's shoulder.

"This way." Raina led them back past the kitchen, but Eden was nowhere to be seen. They went through the gallery and back into the halls, going in the opposite direction of where the people had been dancing.

"How long have you been here?" Nola asked Kieran softly, though she had no real hope Julian and Raina wouldn't hear.

"Since the night after we were banished from the domes." Kieran rubbed the back of his neck. "My father had a few friends in the city, the ones he'd been helping."

"The starving children he had been feeding with the overabundance of the domes," Raina said.

"We went to them," Kieran said, "but I suppose word travels fast out here. In the middle of the night, Emanuel showed up where we were hiding."

"It's not every day a brilliant medical researcher ends up on the streets," Julian said. "Emanuel has been looking for an alternative to Vamp for a very long time." He opened a door and bowed them into a narrower corridor that sloped farther down into the earth.

"He asked my dad to come down here. Promised food, shelter, protection, and all my dad had to do was try to find a way to help people."

"By giving them better drugs?" Nola said. "There has to be a way to make people healthy without making them vampires."

"And what's so wrong with being a vampire?" Raina rounded on Nola. "Is hiding behind glass really better than living underground?"

"Raina," Julian warned.

"If she's going to be around, she should learn how to not insult people who could break her in half." Raina's black eyes gleamed.

A low growl came from Julian.

Raina shrugged and continued down the tunnel.

"I'm not going to be around," Nola said. "One vial. I'm getting one vial to help a little girl, and then I'm done."

Kieran squeezed her hand. "Then you're done."

Raina had stopped walking again, and Nola, too busy looking at Kieran, almost ran into her. His dark hair had fallen over his eyes, but it didn't hide their hurt and fear.

"Kieran—" Nola began, but Julian stepped forward.

"No time for teenage angst, I'm afraid. Cinderella must get home." Julian took Nola by the shoulders, steering her out of the corridor and down a small tunnel with a dead end.

The air in the tunnel was thick and damp. Nola squeezed Kieran's hand, willing herself not to panic at the sheer wall of blackness.

Raina pulled out a heavy key attached to a long chain that had been hidden inside her black leather top. In the darkness of the tunnel, Nola didn't notice the door until Raina reached for the keyhole.

The lock gave a heavy *thunk* as Raina turned the key.

Where she had only been able to see shadowed wall before, cracks of moonlight now split the darkness. Cool, crisp air flooded the hall as the door opened.

"Up you go." Julian pointed to a set of metal stairs.

Nola glanced at Kieran who nodded, and began climbing the metal steps. She expected the stench of the river, or the haze of the city to greet her, but instead, the air smelled like wood and decaying leaves.

A pool of light bathed the top of the steps. Nola reached her hands out, expecting to feel metal or concrete, but her hands met wood. Light crept in through a crack large enough for her to climb through. She turned sideways and slid out into the forest. She looked behind to see Raina climbing out of the tree after her.

No leaves clung to the branches. There would be no reason to look at the tree twice. Kieran climbed out of the vertical slash in the trunk. It looked like the tree had been split by lightning or time. The gap in the bark didn't seem large enough for a person to fit through until Julian emerged from the opening.

"Onwards?" Julian asked.

Nola's gaze followed him as he started up the hill toward the glittering domes, rising just above them.

"What?" Nola said, her feet not moving as she glanced from the tree to her home.

"I know, I know," Julian said, shaking his head, laughter bouncing his voice. "It is a bit passé to have a secret entrance hidden in a tree. However, I find when one becomes the stuff of legend, one might as well embrace the whole fantastical existence. I prefer to write myself into an unlikely fairytale rather than accept my fate is a horror story."

"But it's right here. There's an entrance right here!" Nola shouted before clapping a hand over her mouth.

They stood silent for a moment.

Nola listened for the sounds of guards coming to search the night but couldn't hear anything beyond the pounding of her own heart.

"I was almost killed getting to Nightland tonight," Nola finally whispered. "And you mean to tell me I could have just climbed into a tree and found out Kieran wasn't dead in twenty minutes? Skipping entirely over nearly being killed three times?"

"We couldn't allow that." Raina grabbed Nola's arm, dragging her up the hill toward the domes.

"Why not?" Nola yanked her arm from Raina. "You want me to sneak around and steal things for you, but you couldn't let me use a short cut?"

"It may be hard for you to understand"—Raina tossed her hair, her fingers twitching as though aching to reach for her knife—"but it's just as hard for a vampire to trust a Domer as it is for a Domer to trust a vampire. We couldn't just let Kieran tell his little girlfriend all our secrets, even if he did think you had an actual soul."

Julian hissed, silencing Raina.

"Fine," Nola said. "But if I had died, how long would it have taken you to find someone else who could get you the medicine?"

"If we'd known you would be more useful than the I-Vent, perhaps we could have arranged a parade to escort you to Nightland." Raina took a step toward Nola, her hand draping over the hilt of her knife. "Then again, showing someone who is going to betray you the second they get inside their cozy little domes an easy way into the only safe place you have is a sure way to get all of Nightland slaughtered."

"Enough," Kieran said, stepping between Raina and Nola. "I'll take her the rest of the way."

Raina opened her mouth to argue, but Julian spoke first. "We'll wait for you here, Kieran. Shout if you need us."

Kieran put a hand on the back of Nola's waist, guiding her up the hill.

"This is crazy," Nola said.

"You can do it," Kieran said. "I know you, Nola. You'll be all right."

"No, not just the medicine." Nola ran her hands through her hair, her tangled curls snagged on her fingers. "Vampires, and werewolves, and zombies. This isn't how the world is supposed to be."

"The world is broken," Kieran said. "We broke the planet. Is it so hard to believe the planet broke us right back?"

"But it's all legends, story stuff." Nola tripped over a root.

Kieran wrapped his arm tightly around her waist, steadying her.

Nola looked away from the worry creased on his forehead, blinking in the darkness, trying to focus her tired eyes on the uneven ground. "All I wanted to know was if you were alive. And now..."

"I'm fine," Kieran said. "And now you have the chance to do some real good. Don't forget, Nola, people living in domes was once story stuff, too. We can't choose which stories come true and which stay stories. None of us are that strong."

They were almost to the domes now. The sun had barely begun to paint the night sky gray. Soon the workers would be up, and then the new shift of guards would take up their posts.

Kieran stopped at the last of the trees in the forest. "I don't think I should go any farther."

"They might catch you."

"I might not be strong enough to leave." He touched the ends of Nola's hair and then her cheek. "Be careful."

"I'll see you tomorrow." Nola nodded. She walked out into the field, forcing herself not to look back, knowing Kieran would be watching her.

She half-expected guards to be waiting by the loose pane of glass. Or an alarm to sound as she crawled inside. She crept through the trees and back out onto the stone path as the gray light from the sky turned orange.

She peered through the glass, down over the forest and thought she saw a flicker of movement, but there was no way to know. Back into the empty house and up to her bed. She pulled the I-Vent from her pocket and took a deep breath, letting the metallic taste fill her mouth as her eyes drifted shut and she tumbled into sleep.

CHAPTER ELEVEN

The faint ringing of PAM's bells dragged Nola from sleep. Her head pounded as she tried to sort through everything that had happened the night before. The scent of the damp tunnels clung to her tangled hair. Her shoes were still on, and she clasped her I-Vent in her hand.

It wasn't a dream. There is a tunnel in the woods that leads to a den of vampires living under the city. Kieran is with them.

I've agreed to help them.

"Good Morning," PAM's voice said as soon as Nola climbed out of bed. "Reminder: Today, Dr. Kent will be returning home. Morning lessons will be in the Aquaponics Dome. This evening—"

"Thank you, PAM," Nola said, cutting the computer off. She didn't care what was happening in the domes that evening. Her mind couldn't move past the medical storage unit three stories underground.

Nola went to the shower, turned the water on as hot as she could stand and scrubbed the filth and stench of the city off her skin.

Does Kieran have hot water or soap?

Nola shut off the water, pressing her face to the cool ceramic wall. The shower, the warm fluffy towel. It all suddenly felt too extravagant to be allowed.

"You can't save everyone. Just get the medicine."

She turned the water back on and rinsed her hair. Normal. She had to look normal. Like this was any other day.

Mr. Pillion droned on, his voice dulled by the moss and heavy tank glass in the Aquaponics Dome. He spoke in a soothing, calm tone about the effects of algae blooms on fish populations.

Nola hated the Aquaponics Dome. The class was seated in the dug-down section of the dome, eye-level with the tanks of fish.

Mr. Pillion coughed loudly.

Nola sat up straighter, aware of his eyes on her.

"As the fish waste feeds the plants, the plant waste feeds the fish," Mr. Pillion continued. "What we really need to think about is what plants and fish mesh best together in this type of symbiosis, and which plants and fish can best contribute to the dietary, medicinal, and preservation goals of the domes."

The fish smelled terrible, but it was dark and warm by the tanks—a nice place to sleep. The fish swam in slow circles under the roots of the plants.

Nola didn't feel herself slipping into sleep, but her eyes flew open at a sharp kick in the shins from Jeremy.

"Magnolia," Mr. Pillion said, his eyebrows furrowed in concern, "are you feeling quite well?"

Nola sat up straight and smiled. "I'm fine. Just tired. Sorry, Mr. Pillion, it won't happen again."

"Perhaps we should send you to the clinic." Mr. Pillion frowned. "Just in case."

Nola chewed the inside of her lips. Being sent to the clinic would take hours. And if they thought she was sick, they would place her in isolation. She would never be allowed to visit her mother in her lab if the doctors thought there was any chance of her being contagious.

"Really," Nola said. "I just couldn't sleep last night." Her mind raced for an answer. "I don't like being by myself in the house."

Mr. Pillion gave her a sympathetic look. "Of course." He nodded and turned back to the screen where he was working through a list of extinct ocean species.

Some of the students still stared at Nola. She kept her eyes on the board. She never would have been left alone before her father was killed. Before Kieran and Dr. Wynne were banished. She could feel their sympathy radiating toward her. Nola bit the inside of her lip hard, blinking back the tears stinging the corners of her eyes.

"Unfortunately, some species such as Blue Whales were too large for an attempt at their preservation even to be made," Mr. Pillion said.

The whales had been left out in the ocean to fend for themselves. The tiniest algae killed the largest mammal. The injustice of it burned hot in Nola's chest.

But where could we have put a whale?

The end of lesson chimes sounded in the hall. Nola threw her things into her bag and was first to the door. Her mother should be here by now. If her mother behaved as she always had, she would already be in her lab, carefully checking each specimen and experiment to be sure everything was perfect.

"Nola." Jeremy caught up to her and took her hand, easily matching her quick pace. "Are you sure you're okay?"

Jeremy twined his fingers through hers. Nola's heart caught in her throat. Last night she had been walking with Kieran through the dark in a place she should never have been. And now she was going to steal from the domes. She looked up into Jeremy's eyes. Brown eyes as dark as Eden's.

"I'm fine." Nola pulled her hand away, pretending she didn't see the hurt in Jeremy's eyes as she stepped back. "I'm going to go say hi to my mom. Will you let Mrs. Pearson know where I am if I'm late?"

"Sure."

Nola turned and walked down the hall before Jeremy could say anything else.

Her mother's lab was located three floors below the normal tunnels. The research labs were some of the most important parts of the domes, so they were buried deep underground, far out of reach of storms or riots.

Nola went down the first flight of stairs. Offices branched off in either direction, all lit by sun-mimicking bulbs to make sure no one suffered from lack of light while they worked through the day.

There were no lights like this in the vampire tunnels.

Are sun-lights enough like the real sun to make Raina suffer?

Nola shook her head, banishing thoughts of places she should never have seen. But the clearer her thoughts became, the more the pressure of the earth weighed down upon her.

She descended another flight of stairs to where the food and supplies were stored and where those deemed fit for only menial tasks labored.

Then down the final flight of stairs. Nola's chest tightened, even worse than it had breathing the outside air the night before. Guards stood at either end of the hall, protecting the researchers behind their shiny white doors.

One of the guards nodded at her, not bothering to ask the reason for Nola's visit. She came down to the labs often. If she was going into botany, she needed to know as much as possible, even if the depth of the labs made her ill. She had almost begged to go into transportation just so she would never need to descend the steps to the laboratory. But choosing a path outside botany would have killed her mother. Nola would study plants and how to save the world. It was the only path her mother could accept.

Her mother's figure moved on the other side of the frosted glass of the laboratory door. Nola knocked lightly.

"Yes." Her mother's brusque voice cut through the glass.

Nola peeked her head into the lab. "Hey, Mom."

"Magnolia," her mother said after pausing for a moment, as though trying to figure out who would be calling her *Mom*. "What do you need?"

"I just wanted to say hi, see how the conference was." Nola stepped into the room as her mother began typing away on the computer.

"The conference was fine." Her mother moved toward a tray of cooled samples on the table. "We agreed to institute a new policy that will double food production."

"That's amazing," Nola said. "With that much food, we could actually bring produce to the Charity Center."

"Don't be foolish," her mother said. "The excess space in the greenhouses will be used for further plant species preservation. Just because you can't eat a plant doesn't mean we should allow it to be wiped off the face of the earth."

"I'm sorry," Nola murmured.

"No." Her mother sighed, running her hands through her short hair. "I didn't mean to snap. The conference was good." She sank down into her office chair, massaging her temples. "We're going to be converting one of the domes for tropical preservation this year. We're bringing in a new batch of rain forest species, which is truly exciting. Something I've been fighting for since I got this job."

"Then, what's the matter?" Nola perched on her mother's desk.

"Something went wrong with the seed samples while I was gone." Her mother waved a hand at the tray.

Nola leaned over, examining the dishes of seeds. The outsides had cracked where tiny stems had tried to break through, but the green had faded, replaced by withered brown.

"I was trying to see how short the cold simulation could be," her mother said. "The heat at the end of the cycle was too high and fried the seedlings. And I have no idea what went wrong with the program."

"I'm sorry." Nola pulled her mother into a hug.

"It's fine, I just need to—"

"Get back to work," Nola finished for her mother. "I'll see you at home."

Nola walked back out the door and into the hallway. The guards didn't even look to see who had come out of the lab.

Sweat slicked Nola's palms, her heart pounded in her chest.

I won't even make it to the door before they know something is wrong.

Two doors down. All she had to do was enter two doors down. She exhaled and willed her shoulders to relax.

She wiped her palms on her pants and pushed the seed storage door open.

She glanced at the guards, but their backs were still toward her. She slipped inside, shutting the door silently behind her.

Nola's breath rose in a cloud in front of her. Even with the adrenalin pumping through her veins, she began to shiver. The room had been built to keep the rows upon rows of seeds hibernating. Saving thousands of species from extinction.

It had always seemed strange to Nola that the Dome Council didn't place more guards on seed storage. To the Kents, this was the greatest wealth of the domes.

Someday, years from now, when the water had begun to clear and the air was pure again, people would leave the domes. They would spread out around the world to begin again. And these were the seeds they would take with them.

Nola wanted to stay, read every name on every tray and picture what the plants would look like when they had grown. But this room was not where the answers for Eden lay. Blowing heat onto her hands, Nola walked to the end of the room before turning and heading to the back corner.

There it was, just where Julian had said it would be; a grate at the base of the wall, as high as Nola's waist and just as wide. It was bigger than she had thought it would be, and the faint light of the medical storage room filtered through from the other side. It was only three feet. Less than that really.

Nola knelt and pulled out a thin strip of metal, sliding it into the crack at the edge of the grate, gently prying it away from the wall. She stopped every few seconds, listening for footsteps or the *whoosh* of the door swinging open. But as the grate slid into her hands, no sound of panic came—no running feet, no alarm. Taking a deep breath, Nola crawled into the wall. Her hands trembled. She could leave the other side of the grate off. Leave an exit from the cramped darkness. But if someone came in, they would spot the hole in the wall.

Nola grasped the slats of the grate, feeling them cut into her skin as she pulled the metal into place. Her breath came in shallow gasps. The airshaft opened above her, leading to the next floor. Cold air blew on her, coming from stories above, going through filter after filter to get down to her. Nola turned to the other grate, her whole body shaking from cold and panic. She pushed against the metal, but it didn't budge. She leaned her body into the grate, but it refused to move.

"Please, please just open," Nola whispered, twisting to push on the grate with her feet. A whine of metal on metal echoed around the vent as the grate moved a fraction of an inch. Nola froze, waiting for one of the guards to come running into the room, searching for what had made the noise. But the hum of the air system was the only sound.

"Open dammit." She gave the grate two kicks, and it popped out, hitting the floor of the medical storage room with a clatter.

Nola dragged herself into the room and lay on the ground, gasping at the dim ceiling lights overhead. Again, she waited for the pounding of guards' boots as they ran to arrest her. To throw her out into the world. But there was nothing.

She pushed herself to her knees, searching the room. Where there were rows of shelves in seed storage, here there were glass-fronted cabinets, each labeled with its contents. Nola pictured where Julian had pointed on the map. She pushed herself up onto her shaking legs and walked along the back wall. The vials were classified by type. Names Nola didn't understand.

It should be Kieran down here, climbing through airshafts and stealing medicine.

He would know what all the names meant and be brave enough not to fear the guards.

She reached the cabinet in the far corner. Nola didn't hesitate as she opened the glass door. Fog blossomed on the glass at the heat of her hand.

Pataeris. Sitting right on the shelf. Nola picked up the vial. She expected an alarm to sound. Or for PAM to reprimand her loudly. But there was no noise. No hint of danger.

Nola slipped the vial into her pocket and sprinted back to the grate. Back through the darkness and into seed storage. She could be aboveground in ten minutes. She would see the sun. Nola crawled into the shaft and jammed the grate shut behind her, ignoring the sting as the metal dug into her fingers. With a grind and a tiny *thunk*, the grate was back in place. Nola twisted to the other grate as a familiar voice said, "What the hell was that?"

CHAPTER TWELVE

Nola froze as footsteps came closer to the grate.

"It sounded like the ventilation unit," a man's voice said.

There was an angry murmur before Nola's mother's voice came loud and clear. "I lost an entire tray because the computer mishandled the climate settings on my experiment. That same computer also monitors the climate settings in this room. Correct?"

Nola could picture her mother's face. Eyebrows raised, nostrils flared.

"Yes," the man said. "PAM monitors both systems."

"And PAM is malfunctioning," Nola's mother growled. "So go get every climate control and computer tech down here and get this fixed before we lose every seed we have!"

Angry footsteps pounded away toward the door. Nola could see a pair of thick black boots through the slats of the grate. She held her breath. If he bent down, he would see her.

After a few seconds, the man walked away. Straining her ears, Nola heard the door *whoosh* shut behind him. He would be back.

Back with people who needed to inspect the vents. Nola looked at the other grate. She could go hide in medical storage, but for how long? They would need to check the temperature in there, too.

I'm trapped.

Nola leaned against the metal inside the shaft. She could crawl out now, tell them what she had done, and beg for mercy. They would want to know who the medicine was for.

What if they trace it back to Kieran? And Eden. Wide-eyed little Eden.

Nola opened her eyes. There was another way.

She looked up into the darkness above her. How far up was it to the next floor? Ten feet, maybe twelve? And how long before the man came back?

Nola swallowed and took a deep breath. It was no different than climbing onto her roof. Except for the darkness, metal walls, and tight space. Not to mention the possibility of being banished from her home.

She placed her hands on either wall. Her sweaty palms slipped on the smooth metal. But the walls were close. Close enough for her to balance her weight as she lifted one foot and then the other onto the walls. Although the metal of the airshaft moved with a heavy clunking sound as she pressed against it, Nola didn't stop. It didn't matter if a guard heard. If she stopped, she would be caught. Her pulse thundered in her ears as she climbed, gaining mere inches in height with each step. Her arms shook, her legs cramped, but she couldn't stop.

Kieran.

She took a step.

Kieran will come tonight, and he'll take the medicine to Eden.

Another step.

Once Eden is well, she can grow up strong.

Another step.

Then she'll take ReVamp.

Nola's grip faltered, and she slid down an inch. She jammed her arms into the walls as hard as she could.

Shadows moved above. A foot higher, and she would be to the next level. Nola inched up to the grate. Through the latticed metal, she could see rows of bunks. The guards' housing. And on the other side an office, with the only visible chair empty.

Her fingers shaking, Nola dragged herself onto the ledge by the office, and with the last ounce of energy her legs could muster, kicked the grate away. Gasping and shaking, she threw herself onto the office floor.

Nola lay on the carpet, her eyes closed, trying to convince her heart it should try to keep beating. She waited for a voice to yell —someone to scream at the girl lying on the floor. But there was nothing.

After a minute, Nola opened her eyes. The office was small and empty. A desk and a chair sat in front of a tower of drawers. A faint humming filled the room. Still shaking, Nola pushed herself to her feet, searching for the source of the sound. It couldn't be an alarm. Not with a noise that steady.

A picture of Captain Ridgeway with Gentry and Jeremy perched on one corner of the desk. The Captain wore civilian clothes, and all three of them smiled broadly. Jeremy was shorter than Gentry, so the picture must have been a few years old at least. Nola reached for the picture, wanting to study the normality of it.

The humming stopped her. It came from the drawers. Nola placed her hand on the metal tower. It was cold, like the cabinets below.

Glancing at the office door, Nola quietly fitted the grate back into the wall and opened the buzzing cabinet.

Tiny vials lined the cold drawer. Like the one in her pocket but filled with deep black fluid.

"I don't think it's the vents." The voice traveled up the shaft.

Nola snapped the drawer shut, tearing toward the door. She turned the handle and pulled the door open just a crack. There was no one in sight, though she could hear voices in the distance. Nola ran her hands over her hair in a hopeless attempt to smooth down her curls, and stepped into the hall.

She walked slowly and deliberately, hoping no one would notice the dust on her clothes.

Two men came out of the barracks. They looked Nola over before one elbowed the other and winked at her. The two men laughed softly as they went down the hall.

Nola blushed. They thought she was down here with a guard.

At least they haven't arrested me. Yet.

Half-running, she sped down the hall and up the stairs. She turned a corner and slammed into a group of terrified looking people.

"Sorry." Nola reached for the vial in her pocket before she could stop herself.

If the three she'd run into noticed anything strange, it didn't show as they murmured their apologies and continued toward seed storage. All three wore maintenance uniforms and anxious looks on their faces. They should be worried if Lenora blamed them for the lost seedlings. Nola waited until the workers were out of sight then sprinted the rest of the way up to the atrium.

Nola staggered at the bright light and fresh clean air of the atrium. She wanted to sit on the floor and cry. She was out of the dark and aboveground. The bright green leaves on the trees rustled as the vent blew out air. They were running harder than usual, probably testing the system. That was good. Nola nodded to herself. The more air through the vents, the less likely anyone would notice sweaty handprints.

"Nola!" a voice called across the atrium.

Nola froze, unsure whether to run or not, then finally settled on turning to see who had shouted for her.

"Nola!" Jeremy said again as he ran toward her.

The people who had been enjoying the calm of the atrium scowled at him as he passed.

"Where have you been?" he said as he reached her. He wasn't even out of breath. All of his preparation for guard training was paying off.

"Nola?" he said again, this time with concern in his voice as he took her shoulders.

"Yes?" Nola said.

"You missed our time in the greenhouse," Jeremy said.

She had been gone longer than just lunch. Mrs. Pearson would want to know where she had been.

"I went to see my mom," Nola said. "One of her experiments went wrong, she was upset..."

"And you ran for it?"

That was right. More or less.

Nola nodded.

"I'm sorry," Jeremy said, brushing the sweaty hair from Nola's face. "It must have been some run."

Nola tried to smile at his joke.

Jeremy took her hand and led her down a side path, away from the still glaring bystanders. He stopped under the low-hanging branches of a tree, out of sight of the rest of the atrium.

"Are you sure that's all that's wrong?" Jeremy said softly. "Because you could tell me. Whatever's wrong, whatever's bothering you, you can trust me. You know that, right?"

"I do."

"It's just," Jeremy began, looking down at Nola's hand clasped in his, "I'm here for you. If you were worried about being alone when your mom was away, I could've, I mean, we could've spent time together. Because I want... I want to be with you, Nola. All the time."

Jeremy's hand stroked her hair, then rested on the back of her neck. And he was kissing her. Gently, he pulled her in close, lifting her up so she stood on her toes. His heart pounded so hard the beats resonated through her chest. Nola froze as something in her pocket pressed against Jeremy's hip.

She gasped and took a step back.

"Nola." Jeremy reached toward her.

She pulled her hand away from him without knowing she had moved.

"I'm sorry," Jeremy said, his face red and his eyes filled with hurt. "I thought, I thought you felt the same as me."

Nola's mind raced as she tried to think of feelings beyond fear. The vial in her pocket burned her leg as though it were on fire. Surely Jeremy could see the flaming vial, the proof of her betrayal.

He knows what I did.

"Just forget it," Jeremy said. "Forget I ever... It won't happen again. But I meant what I said. If you need me, I'm here." He turned and walked down the path.

She should let him go, get the vial back home, and wait there for Kieran. Jeremy was disappearing through the branches.

"No." Nola ran after him, taking his hand.

He turned to look at her, his eyes bright and brow furrowed.

"Forget this happened," Nola said. Her mouth had gone dry. She didn't know what she was saying as the words came tumbling out. "Forget you kissed me and I was a sweaty mess who can't manage to think right now."

Jeremy nodded. Pain still filled his face.

"But try it again," Nola said. "Not today. But sometime."

Nola turned and ran through the atrium. She needed to get away before Jeremy asked questions she couldn't answer.

Back through the tunnel and into Bright Dome. She had already missed class. There was no point in going back. There would be no more trouble for missing evening lessons. Up the walk and into her home, Nola shut the door behind her, leaning against it and panting.

She closed her eyes. She had the medicine. She'd finished her job. Now all she had to do was wait for tonight and Kieran would come for the vial. But Jeremy had kissed her. Nola slid down to sit on the floor, trying hard not to think of Jeremy kissing her. Of his warm arms around her.

There were more important things to worry about than if she wanted to be kissing Jeremy in the atrium right now. She slipped her fingers into her pocket and pulled out the tiny vial. She held it up, and the light shone through the orange liquid. There was so little in the tube.

Is this really all it takes to save a little girl's life?

Nola pushed herself to her feet and climbed the steps to her room, absentmindedly grabbing a bowl full of fruit along the way.

Setting the vial on her desk, Nola popped a sweet grape into her mouth. How desperate would you have to be to take Vamp and give up food like this? Nola pulled her drawer out from her desk and set it on her bed. Vial in hand, she reached all the way to a tiny recess at the very back. Carefully, she slid the drawer back into place. It was as though the vial had never existed.

Nola curled up in bed, staring at the drawer. The sun hadn't set yet. It would be hours before Kieran came. Her arms and legs burned. Fatigue muddied her brain. Slowly, her eyes drifted shut.

Darkness filled her room when she woke up. The sun had gone down, and the house was quiet.

The dim clock in the wall read well after eleven. Her mother must have been home for a while. Nola moved to sit up but froze as a shadow shifted.

"It's me," Kieran whispered, taking a step into the pale strip of light that came through the window. "I didn't want to startle you."

"It's okay," Nola whispered, pushing herself to her feet. "I got the vial."

Kieran took a deep breath, catching Nola's hands as she reached for the drawer and pulling her to his chest.

"I thought they'd caught you." Kieran pressed his lips to her forehead. "I was watching the domes. People were coming in and out, looking at the air vents."

"There was something wrong with the climate control." Nola rested her cheek on Kieran's chest. "I had to climb up the vent. I ended up in the Guard barracks."

Kieran pulled away to look into her eyes. "I'm so sorry, Nola. I never should have let Emanuel get you involved."

"He wants to save his daughter." Nola shrugged. "He needs the medicine."

"*Eden* needs the medicine." Wrinkles formed on his forehead. "I won't let Emanuel ask you to do something like that again. It's too dangerous."

"It's fine." Nola laid her fingers on his lips. They were soft, and his breath was warm.

"Nola." He took a step forward. And he was kissing her.

Her knees went weak, but his arms locked around her, holding her tight. Her heart raced as he gently parted her lips with his own.

"Kieran," she murmured, lacing her fingers through his hair.

Kieran froze and backed away, leaving Nola swaying on the spot.

"I have to go," Kieran said, his voice hoarse.

"Now?" Nola stepped in front of the door.

"I live on the outside," Kieran said. "You live in here. What are we supposed to do?"

"I don't know." The rush of heat drained from Nola's body, leaving a cold numbness in its wake.

Kieran took her hands in his. "The hardest part about leaving the domes was losing you." He ran his fingers over her cheek. "But I can't have you. I can't come in here. And I won't"—he cut Nola off before she could speak—"let you leave the domes to find me."

"I miss you." Tears spilled from her eyes, leaving warm tracks running down her cheeks.

Kieran brushed her tears away with his thumb. "I have to go. You know I'm right."

"Stay," Nola whispered. "Just for a little while." She lay down on the bed, pulling Kieran down with her.

She curled up next to him, resting her head on his chest. His heart beat slowly under her ear.

"When will I see you again?" Nola murmured.

Kieran tightened his arms around her, and she knew his answer.

Never.

Nola clung to his shirt, willing time to stop passing so he would never leave.

"Sleep, Nola," he whispered. "Just sleep."

Soon, she had drifted away to the slow rhythm of his heartbeat.

The sun streaming through the windows woke Nola with a gasp the next morning. She sat up, looking for Kieran, but her room was empty. There was no mark on the bed where he had been—if he had even been there at all.

"Kieran," Nola whispered, opening her closet. Her clothes hung in an undisturbed row. She turned back to her room. The fruit bowl sat empty on her desk.

Nola yanked the drawer free, letting it clatter to the floor. She felt into the back corner. The vial was gone. But something small had taken its place.

A slip of paper wrapped around something hard. Nola unfurled the paper and found a little charm. A tiny tree, delicately carved out of wood. Nola held the charm up to the light. A barren tree with a split on one side, a perfect copy of the tree that hid the forest entrance to Nightland.

Nola looked down at the paper. At the note in Kieran's untidy scrawl.

. . .

I'm always yours. Be well.

Nola sank to the floor. He was gone. Kieran Wynne had left the domes. Again.

CHAPTER THIRTEEN

"Nola," her mother's voice came through the door. "Are you awake?"

"Yeah," Nola said, forcing her voice to sound normal, like she hadn't just lost her best friend.

Again.

Nola's mother poked her head through the door. "Good. I was worried when I came home last night and you were already asleep."

"I'm fine," Nola said. "Just tired, really tired."

"Well, come on down. I brought some treats from Green Leaf." Her mother winked and left.

The attendees of Green Leaf always brought food with them —rare fruits that were only grown in their own domes. Nola's stomach rolled in disgust.

Kieran had stolen a bowl of grapes. She could picture him, Dr. Wynne, and Eden sharing the fruit. They were probably the only people in Nightland who could eat it. And they would sit in the kitchen, savoring every bite. While she ate papayas and pomegranate seeds.

Nola went to the bathroom and looked in the mirror. Her

curls surrounded her face like a tangled lion's mane. The dark circles under her eyes made her look as ill as an outsider.

Her hands shook as she splashed cold water onto her face.

She swallowed the scream the smell of the soft, clean towel sent to her throat.

Gripping the edge of the sink, she stared into the mirror. "You've done your part, Magnolia. It's over."

She picked up the comb and tore it through her hair on her way to the kitchen. She didn't care about the pain as she brushed away the last of the filth from the vents. Had it not been for the tiny tree in her pocket, it would have been as though it had never happened at all.

Nola ate her breakfast silently as her mother griped about the subpar maintenance of the cooling system.

"It's pathetic really." Lenora sipped her tea. "We're trying to preserve the resources the world has given us, and they look at me like I'm overreacting when they endanger our seed supplies. Like I'm worried *I* might overheat."

"Right." Nola nodded.

Has Eden taken the medicine yet?

"And I'll be busy enough as it is without having to worry about faulty cooling systems." Lenora took the empty plates from the table and set them in the sink. "We're going to have to start working on the greenhouse consolidation within the next few days if we're going to get the rainforest dome prepped for planting by the end of the month."

"Right."

How long will it take for the Pataeris to take effect?

"Well, I'll see you tonight." Lenora walked out the door without looking back.

"Have a good day, Mom," Nola murmured to the empty house. "I kissed two boys yesterday and stole dome medicine to save a vampire's kid. See you tonight."

Nola grabbed her tablet and headed out of the house. Dark

clouds loomed over the horizon. A deep green tint shaded the sky. Acid rain would be falling on the city in a few hours, burning anyone who strayed outside. Destroying any hope for unprotected crops.

"First acid rain of the year," a voice came from over Nola's shoulder. Gentry Ridgeway limped toward her. "It'll make things worse in the city. A few people had managed to grow a bit of food but—" she shrugged.

The growers would have to start over again.

"How are you?" Nola asked, looking from the cut on Gentry's forehead to the brace on her leg.

"I'll be fine." Gentry blew a bit of her short, blond hair away from her eyes. "Busted leg and a cut-up head. Dad just likes to overreact and tell everyone in the domes I got banged up."

"He worries about you."

"And I worry about Jeremy." Gentry limped a step closer to Nola. "Look, I try not to get involved in my baby brother's life. He's a good kid. He'll be a great guard. And for some reason, he's decided he's head over heels for you."

Heat leapt into Nola's cheeks.

"I don't know what happened between you two yesterday, and quite frankly I don't care," Gentry pressed on, "but I think we can both agree Jeremy is the nicest guy you're going to be able to find in this place. Right?"

"Jeremy's great," Nola said.

"Add that to the fact that he actually likes you, and I see you as one really lucky girl." Gentry pulled herself up to her full height, seeming to tower over Nola. "So, whatever you said that got him all confused yesterday, fix it. I don't care what you have to figure out, or how you have to do it. That boy would walk through fire for you."

"I didn't—I never," Nola pressed her fists to her temples, trying to squeeze all her thoughts together into something that made sense.

"I know you never tried to get him to go all crazy for you, but it happened," Gentry said. "And I don't want to see him hurt. So, make a choice and stick to it. You're a nice girl, Nola. You should get a nice guy. This isn't Romeo and Juliet. This is the domes. You pick someone, and you build a life."

"I'm seventeen," Nola said. "Jeremy is wonderful, but I just—"

"Don't explain anything to me. If you don't want Jeremy, that's your deal. But tell him. And don't wait forever to do it."

Nola nodded, tears stinging the corners of her eyes.

"Now get to class before Jeremy freaks out and thinks you're avoiding him."

Nola nodded and walked down the stone path.

Jeremy would be waiting for her in class. Waiting to make her laugh. Wanting to hold her hand. Offering a world of safety and sunlight, far away from the darkness of Nightland.

CHAPTER FOURTEEN

It had taken nearly three weeks to rearrange the plants in the Amber Dome to make more room for the crops from the Leaf Dome. Classes had been cancelled since all the students were needed to help transfer the fragile plants. If something went wrong and the crops were lost, the food supplies of the domes would disappear with them. All nonessential workers had been assigned to the delicate task.

The days were a blur of work—digging, sorting, and planting until the light became too dim. The domes had become a frenzy of chaos, perfect for avoiding all the Ridgeways.

Nola's mother had begun work on modifying the Leaf Dome two days before, preparing for the shipment of trees and animals that would arrive from the south domes later in the month. The soil content needed to be altered. Different fertilizers, different acidity. Everything the new rainforest would need to grow.

Sweat beaded on Nola's forehead as she hauled another bag of soil up the stairs to the dome. The air hung heavy with the scent of perspiration and fertilizer. The temperature had been turned up to mimic a tropical climate. The only one who seemed to be enjoying the heat was Nola's mother, standing in the middle of the Leaf Dome, new schematics in hand, shouting orders as plant and seed trays were loaded out of the dome.

"You know," Jeremy grunted, sending Nola stumbling as he lifted the bag she'd been dragging up the last few stairs, "there are, what, ten thousand people living in the city? Don't you think we could pay them to haul the dirt? I mean, we could do the planting, but I'm supposed to be going through the training material before I start guard training. Instead, I'm hauling glorified cow poop."

"We can't have outsiders in the domes." Nola searched for a clean place on her sleeve to wipe her forehead.

"Not even once?" Jeremy smiled cautiously.

"No," Nola said, more forcefully than she had meant to. She took a breath. "It wouldn't be fair to show them everything we have and then kick them right back out into the city." She reached up to the little tree charm that hung around her neck. It would be wrong to show Eden the clean air and bright lights of the domes. Her father couldn't live in the light anyway.

"I'm sorry." Jeremy's brow wrinkled. "It was a joke."

Nola arranged her face into a smile. "I know." She pushed out a laugh, but it sounded tinny in the humid air.

"Do you want to get some water?" Jeremy asked, holding out his dirt-covered hand, reaching for Nola's equally filthy one.

"Sure." Her stomach fluttered as she took his hand.

Water stations had been set up along the sides of the dome. Nola's mother's eyes flicked to them every few minutes, making sure no one dared slack off during the planting.

Dew clung to the outside of the water vat, and dirt from the planters' hands had turned to mud on its surface. Jeremy poured two cold glasses and, holding them both, walked away from the others in line for water.

"Here," Jeremy said, passing the glass to Nola. His fingers closed around hers. A shiver ran up Nola's arm.

She didn't know if it was from the cold of the glass or Jeremy's touch. Nola pulled away, taking a drink and turning to watch the planters.

"Are we okay?" Jeremy asked after a long pause.

"What?"

"I kissed you," Jeremy said.

Nola's breath caught in her chest as she remembered Jeremy holding her tight. The warmth of his body flooding into hers.

"And for the past three weeks you've barely spoken to me."

"I'm sorry." Nola shook her head, not knowing what else to say. She couldn't explain she hadn't been talking to anyone because all she wanted to do was scream. And she couldn't stop obsessing over not knowing if the medicine had saved Eden or if the whole thing had been pointless. And she most definitely couldn't tell Jeremy she was terrified of talking to him because if she said something wrong, Gentry might murder her.

"It's all right. I know," Jeremy whispered, taking Nola's hand in his.

"Know what?" A buzz of panic started at the back of Nola's mind.

He turned her hand over, running his thumb along the lines on her palm. "It's Kieran."

"Kieran?"

He knows. He saw Kieran come through the glass. He saw him come into my house.

"You love him." Jeremy let go of Nola's hand.

"I—what?" The buzzing vanished, leaving Nola blinking at Jeremy.

"You two were together. He got banished. You still love him," Jeremy said. His face was set, not with anger, but determination.

"We were friends," Nola said.

"You dated."

"Only for a few months."

"When they made him leave," Jeremy said, "it was like you broke."

Nola remembered. Crying in her room for days. Barely eating. Not speaking to anyone. Until Jeremy made her, forcing her everyday to become a little more human again. Making her laugh when she thought it was impossible.

And they were back there again.

"He was my best friend," Nola said, "and they took him away. But he, we, it's not like we were going to get married." But was that true? If he had stayed, would they still be together? Would they have been together for years, or for their whole lives?

A life in the sunlight with Kieran by my side.

"He was my friend, too," Jeremy said. "And I don't expect you to forget him."

"He's not dead," Nola snapped.

The workers standing by the cooler glared at her.

"He's not dead," Nola whispered. He was just outside the domes. Through the tree. She gripped the charm at her throat without thought.

"He's gone," Jeremy said. "And he's never coming back." He stepped forward, raising a hand to caress Nola's cheek. "But I'm here. I'm right here, Nola. And I'm not going anywhere."

"Jeremy," Nola whispered.

His hand smelled like soil and life. Like the domes and everything they protected.

"I think we could be something wonderful," Jeremy murmured. "I think we could be happy."

Nola looked into his eyes, and the fear that had clung to her heart for weeks faded away. She raised her hand to hold his as it rested on her cheek. "I think so, too."

Standing up on her toes, she leaned forward and brushed her lips gently against his. Her heart fluttered, and her stomach danced. But the world stayed upright. There was no rabbit hole for her to tumble through like with Kieran.

"Magnolia," an angry voice came from behind her.

Jeremy looked over Nola's head and jumped away from her as though burned.

Nola spun around to see her mother's rigidly angry face.

"Magnolia," Lenora said. "I would have expected you to show a little more respect for work that is so important to the domes. And Jeremy"—she rounded on Jeremy, who suddenly looked smaller than Lenora—"if you expect to join the Outer Guard like your father and your sister, you will have to learn some discipline. Priorities need to be respected. Especially where my daughter is concerned."

Lenora grabbed Nola by the arm and dragged her away. Past the water station, where the people now openly gawked at the Kents, through the planting lines, and to an empty section of the dome.

"Mother," Nola said as the men carrying the planting trays stopped to stare, "I can walk on my own."

"And I can see exactly what you walked into," Lenora spat.

"I'm seventeen," Nola said, yanking her arm away. "I kissed a boy. I shouldn't have stopped working, I'm sorry. But you like Jeremy."

Lenora stopped and glared at her daughter. Nola could read the battle raging in her mother's mind, warring between what she wanted to say and what she knew would be most effective.

"Jeremy has his path, and you have yours," Lenora said, her tone clipped. "You have an obligation to the domes. Above all other things, the domes come first. And *we* believe the best way to preserve the domes is by preserving the plants and people within them. Nothing more, nothing less. Jeremy Ridgeway does not fit into that plan."

Lenora took her daughter's shoulders and steered her to the far corner of the dome. A line of trays lay next to the glass, filled with spinach plants that were past their prime and tomato vines that had stopped bearing fruit for the season.

"Harvest the dirt," Lenora said.

"Dirt?" Nola examined the last few stunted carrots that had been pulled from the soil.

"Get the plants out of the dirt," Lenora said. "Put the plants on the carts for compost. Save the soil in the bins. It's still fertile. It can be used in the new Amber Dome beds once the roots from these plants are gone. When you've done that, you come straight home. You do not speak to anyone. You do not stop anywhere. You are—"

"Grounded," Nola finished for her mother.

"I'm glad you have enough sense left to figure that out." Lenora turned and stalked away, leaving Nola alone with the aging plants.

Darkness had fallen before Nola finally limped up the steps up to Bright Dome. Her back throbbed from spending hours stooped over the plants. Choosing each bit of edible food and sorting it from the dead plants to be composted, laying the food neatly on trays to be sent down to be distributed to the residents of the domes.

The lights blazed in her house as Nola walked up the worn stone path. Nola flicked her eyes up to the stars, giving a silent plea her mother wouldn't want to talk about Jeremy again.

She rubbed the dirt from her hands onto her pants before opening the kitchen door. Holding her breath she counted three seconds of silence. Maybe Lenora had fallen asleep, or better yet, was still locked in her office down in the tunnels.

"Magnolia," Lenora's voice came from the corner, "how long can it possibly take to finish a simple task?"

Nola chewed the inside of her cheek, her fatigue telling her to argue with her mother, her common sense telling her to keep quiet and hope it ended soon. Nola stepped into the bright kitchen and closed the door behind her.

"I asked you a question," Lenora said, stepping in front of Nola and blocking her path up the stairs. "Why has it taken you so long to get home?"

"I came home as soon as I was finished." Nola took a step forward, watching the dirt fall from her clothes onto the polished kitchen floor.

"Why on earth did it take you five hours to sort the trays?" Lenora snapped. "It would have taken a ten-year-old two."

"Then you should have asked a ten-year-old to do it," Nola growled, knowing it was a mistake to have spoken as soon as she saw the lines form around her mother's pursed lips.

"I asked you," Lenora said. "Did you stop to see Jeremy?"

"No." Nola dug her filthy nails into her palms. "I sorted the edibles from the scraps. Got rid of the compost, prepped the food for distribution, and labeled the soil trays for transfer. And yes, that was a lot of work, and yes, I just finished."

Lenora raised an eyebrow. "I never told you to salvage any food. Those plants were past their prime."

"There was still good food," Nola said.

"And it will do just fine as compost." Lenora waved a hand. "If I had wanted it for distribution—"

"You're just going to throw that food away?" Nola asked.

"No, we're going to compost it," Lenora said.

"But it could be eaten." Nola's mind scrambled to grasp her mother's meaning.

"We don't need it," Lenora said, walking back to her computer at the table.

"But the people in the city do," Nola said. "We could send it to them."

"There isn't enough to feed the whole city. It isn't even enough for an afternoon at the Charity Center. I appreciate your extra effort, and your coming straight home, but next time I suggest you pay closer attention to instructions."

"But the food could go to the city." Nola followed her mother to the table. "There are hungry people who need to eat."

"There isn't enough to go around." Lenora didn't look up from her computer. "Besides, the outsiders can take care of themselves. They aren't our concern. They've invented enough drugs to keep themselves plenty occupied without our getting involved."

"Mom, those people out there are dying." Nola shoved her hands through her hair, feeling the dirt crumble into the dark strands. "Even the little kids, all of them are sick. Those drugs they take are the only way they can survive."

"I know that, Magnolia." Lenora lifted her hands from her computer and folded them in her lap. "The people in the city are suffering. Their lives are filled with hardship, want, and pain, which is why we have a moral obligation to help them however we can. The Charity Center is more than enough—"

"Feeding them, what, a few times a month? Each age group only goes to the Charity Center once a month, and we call that helping? That isn't enough. We have good food here you're going to get rid of. We have clean water. We have medicine that can help them. It could save their lives!"

"We don't have enough for all of them," Lenora said, her voice growing sharp. "I know it is a difficult truth to accept. But we don't have enough resources to feed everyone. The greenhouses can only produce enough uncontaminated food to feed the population of the domes."

"Then grow more." Nola paced the kitchen. "Build another greenhouse, get rid of the new tropical plants, increase food production."

"We're trying." Lenora stood and took her daughter by the shoulders, stopping her mid-step. "What do you think the Green Leaf Conference is about? We are trying to secure the future of the human race. We have to preserve our resources—"

"But what about preserving those people?" Angry tears formed in Nola's eyes.

"We're doing our best. Everyone here is working to find a way to save what's left of our planet."

"But what if the person who could figure out how to save us all is stuck out there? What if there's some kid in the city who's smart enough to figure out how to grow enough food that no one will ever be hungry again?" Tears streamed down Nola's face.

"We'll never know." Lenora picked up her napkin and wiped her daughter's face. "I know it's terrible. I wish we could feed everyone, but we can't. The domes aren't about saving this generation. The domes were built to preserve the human race—to protect our DNA and the ability to produce healthy children. So that when we find a way to get rid of the toxins in the air and the water, there will actually be healthy humans left to carry on."

"And what about the people out there dying right now?" Nola choked through her tears.

"If a life boat isn't big enough to save everyone on a ship, that doesn't mean you let all the passengers die. You save as many as you can, and you head for shore." Lenora stared into her daughter's eyes. "It is the only way."

Nola turned away. She couldn't stand to look at her mother anymore.

"Hate me if you want," Lenora said. "It's a terrible truth. But it's one we have to live with. It's the only way we can survive."

"I don't know if I can do that." Nola didn't wait for her mother to say anything. She walked back out the kitchen door, letting it slam behind her.

Rain pounded down on Bright Dome in fierce sheets, the water tinted brown in the dim light. The rain would burn everything in its wake tonight.

How acidic would rain need to be to leave marks like the ones on Desmond's skin?

Nola wanted to run out into the rain. To scream and cry and let the world burn her for living hidden from its pain for so long.

To tell the outsiders there was food and medicine waiting inside the domes.

Nola walked to the gurgling fountain at the center of the dome. Its noise was barely audible over the rain that grew harder by the minute.

Nola stuck her hands into the water, washing away the dirt before splashing her face. The cold water gave her goose bumps wherever it touched her skin. It was cleaner than any of the water they had on the outside. She stood and ran to the stairs, not wanting to be near the fountain anymore. It was too lavish, too selfish.

Her feet carried her down into the tunnel before she could even think where she wanted to go.

CHAPTER FIFTEEN

The Iron Dome was near the very center of the compound, beside the atrium, directly above the barracks. All of the Outer Guard with families lived in that dome with the barracks beneath for unmarried guards. The Iron Dome and the barracks were the only residences where weapons were kept, the only place where metal could shield the glass walls in case of attack.

A guard waited at the top of the stairs to the Iron Dome.

"I'm here to see Jeremy Ridgeway," Nola said before he could ask, hoping the darkness would hide her tear-streaked face.

The guard stared at her for a moment before nodding and letting her pass without another word.

The homes were smaller here. Utilitarian units meant to house soldiers. There were no trees here that could block sight lines. Only low-lying plants were allowed in the Iron Dome. Nola's skin tingled with the feeling of being watched.

Jeremy's house sat on the outskirts of the dome. The only hint that the home belonged to the head of the Outer Guard was its being shaped like a slightly larger shoebox than the others.

Light streamed through the windows of the house, and voices came from the kitchen.

Nola ran a hand over her face as she tried to think. Captain Ridgeway wouldn't like her crying at his door this late at night. Nola crept around to the side of the house, hoping no guards would be lurking in the shadows, ready to shoot her with one of their shiny needles.

Nola knelt, tracing her fingers through the edge of the garden bed, searching for a few pebbles. Carefully, she tossed the handful of stones at Jeremy's window. Nola tensed at the faint clatter of the rocks against the glass. She held her breath, waiting in the dark.

Please don't be in the kitchen, Jeremy.

Jeremy's window slid open and he popped his head out, looking around. He smiled as his gaze found Nola. "Aren't I the one who's supposed to be throwing rocks at your window?"

"I just..." Nola began, but she didn't know why she had needed to see Jeremy, only that she hadn't known where else to go.

"Are you okay?" Jeremy asked, his tone shifting from light to concerned.

Nola shook her head.

She gasped and stumbled back as, in one swift movement, Jeremy vaulted out of his window and landed next to Nola with barely a noise.

"You've been training," Nola said, her voice shaking.

Jeremy didn't answer as he wrapped his arms around her. She laid her head against the hard muscles of his chest. She had never noticed them there before.

He's already becoming one of the elite.

Her breath caught in her throat as she began to cry again.

"*Shh*," Jeremy hushed, petting her hair. "You're okay. I've got you." He held her for a moment in the darkness. Both of them flinched as a barking voice carried from the kitchen.

"Come on." Jeremy threaded his fingers through Nola's, leading her away from the house to a stand of ferns near the wall of the dome. Jeremy dropped down to his knees, hiding his height in the shadows, and pulled Nola to follow.

"What's wrong?" He pushed Nola's curls away from her face. "Is your mom that upset about us?"

"Yes," Nola said before shaking her head. "She is, but that isn't what's wrong."

"Then what is it?" Jeremy took Nola's hand and pressed her palm to his lips. "You can tell me, Nola. Whatever it is, you can trust me."

Nola's mind raced back. The I-Vent, ReVamp, the break in the glass, Kieran. She could tell Jeremy everything.

You wouldn't have to be alone anymore. You wouldn't have to lie anymore.

Jeremy would understand why she couldn't stand her mother or the idea of only saving the chosen few.

"I do trust you." Nola swallowed, tightening her grip on Jeremy's hand.

Light splashed out of Jeremy's front door as five Outer Guard in full city uniform poured out of the house.

Jeremy dove to the side, pulling Nola out of the light and clamping a hand over her mouth.

They waited, frozen and silent until the group disappeared down the dark path.

Nola pulled Jeremy's hand from her mouth. "Why were there Outer Guard in full city uniform in your house?"

"My dad's their boss," Jeremy said, his voice tight.

"Guards only wear those uniforms when they leave the domes," Nola said. "Why would they be hanging out in your house like that? If they're going on patrol, they should be leaving from the barracks."

Jeremy looked to the house. The kitchen door was closed. "My dad doesn't trust the Dome Guard right now."

"Why?" Nola asked. "The Outer Guard and the Dome Guard are the same. They're just an extension of each other."

"You can't tell anyone," Jeremy said. "My dad wouldn't have told me, except I'll be in training next month. And Gentry has been going out with the patrols lately. I started figuring out something was going on."

Nola nodded.

"The Outer Guard have found a den. It's a bunch of Vampers all living underground together." Jeremy glanced back at the house. "The Dome Guard think it's not our business. That the Vampers should be able to do what they like on their side of the river. But the Outer Guard, they're out there on the street every night. The wolf packs running around are bad enough, but that many Vampers, if they decided to come after the domes..."

"We couldn't stop them."

Raina and Julian breaking through the glass. The people from the club coming in search of blood.

It would be a massacre.

"But why would they want to attack us?" Nola said.

"They don't understand what we're doing in here." Jeremy swept his hands up to the glass of the dome. "We're trying to save the world. We live trapped in here for the good of the species."

Trapped in a lifeboat while the rest of the world drowns.

"It's okay." Jeremy pulled Nola to his chest, pressing his lips to her hair. "They're close to figuring out where the den is. Once they do, the Outer Guard will go in—"

"And what?" Nola's mouth went so dry she could barely form the words.

"Neutralize the threat." Jeremy looked deep into Nola's eyes. "I won't let anyone hurt you."

Eden. Tiny little Eden couldn't hurt anyone if she tried.

"What if they don't want to hurt us," Nola whispered, her voice trembling. "What if all they want is to survive? And they have to live underground to protect themselves?"

Jeremy leaned in, brushing his lips against Nola's. "You always want to believe in the good in the world. I think that's why I love you."

Nola forgot how to breathe as Jeremy kissed her, holding her close to his chest. Nola pushed away, falling back onto the grass, her heart racing as her body remembered she needed air.

"Jeremy—"

"Don't say anything now." He stood and reached down, pulling Nola to her feet. "I know it's a lot. But it's true. I love you, Nola." He took her hand, turning it over to kiss her wrist.

Her knees wobbled as tingles ran up her arm.

"And I can wait." Jeremy smiled. "I can wait till you're ready."

A bubble of pure joy washed away all thought. There was nothing in the world but his brown eyes and his smile meant only for her.

The lights in Jeremy's living room flicked off.

Jeremy cursed. "I have to go." He kissed Nola on the top of the head. "I'll see you in the morning."

He ran toward the house and vaulted through his window before Nola could remember why she had come to the Iron Dome.

The food.

She was angry with her mother for not wanting to share the domes' food with the people the Outer Guard were going to attack.

Nola's hands trembled as she reached for the tree pendant at her throat.

Kieran.

If the guards went into the tunnels, they would find Kieran. Nola looked up at the sky. Rain still pounded down on the glass. Did the guards already know about 5th and Nightland? How long would it take them to get there?

Keeping her eyes front, Nola walked back to the guard at the stairs. His helmet and coat hung on the wall next to him.

"Captain Ridgeway wants you at his house," Nola said. Her

voice sounded far away as though someone else were speaking. "He heard someone prowling around."

The guard nodded stiffly before running toward the Ridgeway house. Grabbing the coat and helmet from the wall, Nola bolted down the stairs, not bothering to wonder what the guard would think when Captain Ridgeway told him there had been no prowler.

CHAPTER SIXTEEN

The oversize coat hung down over Nola's hands. But she would need the protection from the rain. She'd already tucked the inner glass to the side. Nola's fingers slid across the outer glass, slipping on the condensation.

"Please just move," Nola whispered. What had been such a simple plan when she took the guard's jacket now seemed impossible.

What if I can't find the tree in the rain? What if the door is locked from the other side?

Gripping the glass, she pulled with all her might, not letting up as she felt a jagged edge slice into her fingers. Finally, the glass moved and she pushed it aside, sucking on the cut. She would have to be more careful putting it back when she came home.

Nola shoved the helmet onto her head. The stench of someone else's sweat flooded her nose, overpowering the acrid scent of the night. Wrapping her hands tightly in the coat, she crawled out into the rain, twisting carefully to replace the glass before standing up and running down the hill.

She didn't bother searching for guards. She wouldn't be able to see them coming through the rain, which pounded down on her coat. She could feel the weight of each drop as it struck the fabric. She had never dreamed rain could have such weight—that each drop would have individual definition.

The sound of her breathing and the rain striking the helmet matched the pounding of her heart as she ran down the hill toward the forest.

Her heel slipped out from underneath her, and before she could try to right herself, she slid down the hill. She screamed as something struck her spine. Digging her bare hands into the mud, she finally stopped, lying on her back. The helmet had somehow stayed on. Rain and mud smeared the visor.

Nola pushed herself up. Tears flowed from her eyes as pain shot from her spine. The skin on her hands burned from the rain. Nola wiped them on her pants, but it was no good. Her hands still stung. She looked back over her shoulder. The dim lights of the domes were barely visible.

Her bed and her shower were at the top of the hill. A doctor who could make the pain in her hands stop was at the top of the hill.

She turned back to the trees, scrambling to her feet. Her ankle throbbed as she walked into the forest. She searched the darkness for a barren tree with a slit she could climb through. But in the rain, all the trees looked the same. Nola glanced back at the domes. She had been able to see Bright Dome when she came out of the tree with Kieran. Squinting through the visor, she tried to make out which dim light was Bright Dome. It was hidden behind the Amber Dome with its wide stance and low ceiling. Nola walked left, closer to the bridge into the city, studying each tree as she went.

A shadow passed in front of her. Nola dove behind the nearest tree, pressing herself into its shadow. Her breath came in quick gasps. The Outer Guard. If they had found the tree, they would find Nightland.

If they find me...

Nola peered around the side of the tree, searching for the moving shadow. And there it was, fifty feet in front of her. The tree that hid the entrance to Nightland. Nola waited for a moment, holding her breath, searching for an Outer Guard in the night. Nothing moved.

Run, Nola, you need to run! the voice inside her head shouted, but her feet wouldn't move.

Ten seconds, Nola. Her father's voice echoed in her memory. *You get ten seconds to panic. Then you're done. That's all you're allowed.*

Nola nodded.

Ten, nine, eight, seven...

What if the Outer Guard were already through the door?

Six, five...

What if they had already found Dr. Wynne's Laboratory?

Four, three...

Kieran.

Nola ran toward the tree, ignoring the pain that shot through her back and the grip of the mud as it tried to steal her shoes. Her fingers closed around the edge of the bark as she pulled herself through the opening.

Crack!

Pain shot through her head before burning cut through her ribs. Blackness overtook her before the scream left her mouth.

CHAPTER SEVENTEEN

Her mouth tasted like dirty cotton. She tried to lick her lips, but her tongue cracked with the movement. She tried to take a breath, but pain shot through her lungs, and a cough caught in her sandpaper-like throat.

She opened her eyes. Spots danced in her vision, blocking out the scene around her. The lights in the room were bright—much, much too bright.

The medical wing. I must be in the medical wing.

But the skin on her hands still burned.

Nola tried to lift her hands to look at them; it felt like sand had filled her arms, making them too heavy to move properly. The skin on her hands was red against the white light.

"Nola," a voice breathed.

Footsteps pounded across the floor, and Dr. Wynne and Kieran hovered over her, their faces blurred.

"Nola." Kieran knelt, taking Nola's hand. The cold of his fingers soothed her skin.

"What—"

"Don't try to speak." Dr. Wynne disappeared from view, coming back with a cup in his hand. "You need to drink."

Kieran lifted Nola's head. She gasped as pain shot through her skull. "Sorry," he whispered before tipping cool liquid into Nola's mouth. It tasted metallic and stale, but it coated her throat and made it easier to breathe. Kieran sat on the bed, lifting Nola to lean against his chest before giving her more of the foul fluid.

"Where am I?" Nola asked after a few sips.

"Nightland," Kieran said.

Nola's mind raced. Back to the tree. To the pain. "But the Outer Guard. They found me."

Dr. Wynne looked at Kieran before speaking. "It wasn't the Outer Guard. It was our guard."

"Why in Hell were you wandering through the woods in a guard's uniform at night?" Kieran said, anger creeping past the concern in his voice. "They thought you were trying to break in. They almost killed you. If they hadn't recognized you, they would have."

"I had to tell you," Nola said, remembering her urgency and coughing in her haste.

Kieran lifted more water to her mouth.

"There's no time." Nola pushed the cup away. "I only have a few hours."

Kieran glanced to his father. "Nola, you've been here for two days."

The bed swayed. Her head spun, blurring the room around her.

Two days. Nola tried to reason through the words. *I've been here for two days.*

"That can't be right." Nola shook her head and the world danced in bright spots.

"Careful." Kieran steadied her as she tipped toward the edge of the bed. "We patched you up as best we could, but you need to be careful."

"They'll know I'm gone." Nola pictured her mother calling for her when she didn't come out of her room in the morning. Did she think Nola had snuck out to be with Jeremy? And Jeremy. What did he think when Nola's mother came searching for her? How long did it take them to figure out she was gone? Had she already been banished in absentia?

"Why on earth did you come out in the rain?" Dr. Wynne pressed something cold and metallic against Nola's forehead. "You could have gotten lost in the storm, or sick from the rain, you aren't used to the toxicity. And then being stabbed on top of it all."

"Stabbed?" Nola asked, remembering a searing pain in her back.

"They thought you were trying to infiltrate Nightland," Kieran said. "They didn't mean to hurt you."

"The Outer Guard." Nola pushed away from Kieran to seize Dr. Wynne's hands. "I have to talk to Emanuel. I have to see him right now."

"Why?" Dr. Wynne said. "I know it must be frightening to be away from the domes for so long, but you're safe here."

"No one is safe here." Nola twisted to throw her legs off the bed. Every muscle in her body ached. "The Outer Guard. They know about Nightland. They're trying to find a way in. They might already know how. You have to get everyone out."

Dr. Wynne and Kieran exchanged silent glances.

"I'll go," Kieran said, lifting Nola and laying her back on the bed. "Stay. Let him take care of you. I'll be right back." He disappeared behind the head of the bed, and the slam of a door shook the room a moment later.

"Well," Dr. Wynne said, sitting next to Nola's bed, "you have a concussion. But you're awake, so a good rest is all we can do for that. The knife didn't go too deep, and thankfully it missed all the really important bits or you would have bled to death before they got you to me. You've been stitched up, and I've given you everything I can to make sure you don't get an infection."

"There's a hole in me?" Nola said, bile burning her throat at the thought.

"Yes, and no." Dr. Wynne took off his glasses and cleaned them on his shirt. "I may have tried something a little... experimental."

"Experimental?"

"I needed to heal the wound as quickly as possible, and we have such limited resources." Dr. Wynne's hands fluttered through the air.

"What did you do?"

"Well, after doing as much as I could"—Dr. Wynne looked at the ceiling—"I gave you a few tiny injections of ReVamp."

Nola's heart raced as though trying to prove its lack of humanity.

"It was all very localized," Dr. Wynne added quickly. "You should have no long term effects. Your body temperature and heart rate are still very normal. And I must say the wound has healed exquisitely. Once you're rehydrated and can get up and moving, I would say you should be just fine in a few days. Maybe less. As I said, it was an experiment. And the rate of healing has been extraordinary."

"So, you didn't make me a..." Nola couldn't bring herself to say the word.

"Vampire?" Dr. Wynne shook his head. "No. Though if you hadn't woken up soon, a full injection may have been the only choice. But it seemed, under the circumstances, that your return to the domes would be infinitely more difficult if you had become a vampire."

"I don't think they'll take me back." Nola stared at her red hands. "I left. I went outside, without permission, to help vampires. I don't think that's the sort of thing the domes will take me back from."

"Don't give up hope yet," Emanuel's voice came from behind the bed.

Nola struggled to sit up, and in a moment Kieran sat beside her, supporting her weight.

"Emanuel," Nola began, the words tumbling out, "the Outer Guard. They know about Nightland. They know there's a huge group of vampires living together underground. They think you're all working together, planning to attack the domes. And they're looking for you. They want to destroy you. And they're getting closer to finding you. They could be at 5th and Nightland right now, trying to break in. You have to get everyone out of here. It's not safe anymore."

Emanuel considered Nola for a moment, his black eyes narrowed. "How do they know about Nightland?"

"I have no idea," Nola said. "But they do."

"How do you know?" Emanuel asked.

"Jeremy Ridgeway." Nola's face flushed.

Emanuel's eyes flicked to her cheeks, and more heat flooded her face.

"His father is the head of the Outer Guard," Nola said. "I saw guards coming out of his house in full uniform. I asked why, and Jeremy told me."

"Why?" Emanuel asked. "Is it common knowledge in the domes?"

"No." Nola shook her head. "Jeremy's father told him about Nightland because Jeremy is joining the Outer Guard next month. And Jeremy told me because"—Nola thought of Jeremy sitting with her in the dark—"because he trusts me."

Kieran stiffened by her side.

"And why did you come to tell us?" Emanuel turned his gaze to the ceiling. "Why did you place warning us over the trust of Jeremy?"

"Because," Nola said, balling her red, scarred hands into fists, "you are good people. It's not your fault you have to live out here. You're doing the best you can. You aren't going to attack the domes, so how could I let the guards attack you? It would be a slaughter. They have weapons—"

"We are well guarded." Emanuel knelt in front of Nola, taking her hands in his own. "We have more protection than the guards can comprehend. But knowing they are coming, we can ensure that when they arrive we can turn them away without unnecessary violence. You have saved lives in coming here, Nola. You were incredibly brave."

"Thank you." The words caught in Nola's throat.

"I will make sure you are not punished for your bravery," Emanuel said. "We will find a way to get you home."

"They won't want me."

"There may be a way. A way that will get you home and save lives in Nightland." Emanuel stood to leave. "Kieran, please see that she has food and fresh clothing. I'll go speak to the others and see what we can think up to save our hero." He nodded to Nola and left.

"I'll be right back," Kieran said, gently squeezing Nola's hand before following Emanuel.

"Well," Dr. Wynne said after a long moment. "Let's check your bandages, shall we?" He pushed his glasses up on his nose. "Lean forward."

It wasn't until that moment Nola realized she wasn't wearing her own clothes. She had been changed into an old hospital gown. It was worn, soft, and tattered around the edges.

Nola winced as Dr. Wynne pulled the sticky bandage from her skin.

"Hmmm," Dr. Wynne murmured as he ran his fingers across her back.

"What?" Nola asked. "Is it infected? Am I becoming a vampire?"

"Not a bit," Dr. Wynne said. "It's even better than I expected."

Nola pushed herself to her feet, tottering for a moment before stumbling to the cracked mirror in the corner of the room. Pulling the robe down over her shoulder, she twisted to see her back in the mirror.

"Careful," Dr. Wynne warned. "You don't want to tear anything that's newly mended."

Then her eyes found it. A red, raised, jagged mark three inches long right under her left shoulder blade.

"You're very lucky you were wearing the guard's coat. Otherwise the knife would have penetrated your lungs. And that"—Dr. Wynne spread his hands—"would have been a very different story."

"It looks like it happened months ago," Nola said, trying to touch the mark.

"She shouldn't be standing," Kieran said as he came back through the door, balancing a plate on top of a pile of clothes.

"I feel better standing." Nola studied her face in the mirror. She looked pale, like she hadn't slept for days, but otherwise healthy. The only marks on her were the scar on her back and the red of her hands.

"You should feel better the more you move." Dr. Wynne smiled. "I gave you another tiny bit of ReVamp this morning." He waved away the frightened look on Nola's face. "You needed it to heal. And as I said, no lasting effects. And the more the drug is circulated, the better you'll recover."

"That's remarkable." Nola rubbed her fingers over the tight red skin on her hands.

"It seemed a bit much," Dr. Wynne said, his brows furrowed, "to give you localized ReVamp injections in your hands just to fix the inflamed skin. The chance for infection is so small, it's really only cosmetic damage, and they can mend that in the domes."

If I ever get back into the domes.

"Thank you." She pushed her face into a smile. "Thank you for saving my life. ReVamp...what it can do is amazing. We don't have anything that can do this in the domes."

"You need to eat," Kieran said, pulling out the desk chair and setting down the plate of food.

"Right." Nola swallowed the lump in her throat. Her stomach rumbled at the sight of food. She hadn't eaten since the domes.

She looked down at the food on the plate. Some sort of chopped vegetables she had never seen before lay next to a hunk of bread and a small bit of meat.

"I know it's not what you're used to," Kieran said, handing Nola a fork as she sat down at the desk, "but it's not bad."

"But will," Nola said, glancing between Kieran and Dr. Wynne, "will it make me sick?"

"This is good food," Dr. Wynne said. "It's the best we have."

"I'm sorry," Nola said. "I didn't mean—"

"It would take years for you to get sick from this," Kieran said. "It may not be dome-pure, but Nightland spends a lot of time finding the best soil we can. We work hard to keep the irrigation water clean. This is better than anything you'll get on the streets."

"Thank you," Nola said. "For sharing." She took a bite of the vegetables, trying not to wrinkle her nose at the metallic taste of the food.

"That's the ReVamp." Dr. Wynne perched on the edge of the desk. "The unfortunate taste should dissipate as you metabolize more food. The meals here really aren't that bad."

"Why do vampires grow food?" Nola choked down another bite.

"For the kids," Kieran said. "For the people in the city who don't have anything to eat."

"Vampires feed people?"

"The ones in Nightland do," Kieran said. "Emanuel doesn't want to keep everyone in Nightland forever."

Dr. Wynne stood, clapping his hands together. "I'm sure Emanuel will be back any minute with a plan to get Nola out of here, and she should be dressed." He walked out of the room, holding the door open for Kieran to follow.

"I'll be right back," Kieran said.

The door shut behind them, leaving Nola alone. She took a bite of the bread, hoping the tinny taste would be different. It wasn't.

She picked up the clothes that had been left for her. Thick black pants and a stitched-together black leather top. Both were worn and patched in places.

Nola dug the heel of her hand into her forehead. She was alive, that was good. They wanted to get her back to the domes, also good. Dr. Wynne was hiding something from her. Badly. Not so good.

CHAPTER EIGHTEEN

She pulled on the clothes without letting herself consider the rough texture of the leather against her bare skin. They had been made for someone larger than her, with muscle and curves Nola lacked.

A knock sounded on the door.

"Are you dressed yet?" Kieran called.

"Yes?" Nola said tentatively, staring at her pale face and leather-clad body in the mirror.

I look like I belong in Nightland.

Kieran came in, not bothering to suppress his laugh as he saw her.

"Thanks." Nola grimaced, taking another bite of the bread and instantly regretting it as the metallic taste flooded her mouth.

"You look great." Kieran ran a hand through his hair. "Just not like you. It's going to take them a while to figure things out. Emanuel has a grand plan, but they still have to iron out the details."

"What kind of grand plan?" Nola pushed the food around her plate, searching for an appetizing bite.

"Emanuel doesn't usually share his plans with me," Kieran said, his face darkening for a moment, "but I trust him."

"What were you saying before, about Emanuel wanting to get people out of Nightland?" Nola looked into Kieran's eyes, seeking a real answer.

"Nothing."

"Then why did your father make you leave?"

Kieran grinned. "You know him so well."

Nola waited in silence.

"There's a lot of land, other places away from the domes," Kieran whispered, his words flowing more quickly as he spoke. "There are places where the soil isn't as bad. Where there isn't a polluted river in the backyard. The domes were built here because they needed the city for laborers. But they abandoned the city as soon as the domes were ready. Why should we sit here waiting to die if there's something better out there?" He stretched his arms to the sky through the dirt above them.

"Why didn't your father want me to know?"

"Emanuel doesn't want the domes to know." Anger crept into his voice. "He's worried they won't want us to build a good place of our own."

"Aboveground?"

"For Eden," Kieran said. "The vampires can't stay in the light."

"But the food," Nola asked. "Do you grow it underground?"

"I was sort of hoping you'd ask." Kieran's eyes gleamed with excitement. "I think you'll be amazed with what we've done." He stood, walking toward the door before reaching a hand back to Nola. "Come with me?"

Nola stood and took his hand, not caring where he led her.

They were in the same part of Nightland where she had seen Eden. They passed the kitchen, but the little girl with the big brown eyes was nowhere to be seen.

"Eden," Nola asked as they slipped into the gallery, "is she—"

"She's fine." Kieran beamed. "The medicine helped. She can

breathe now. I actually had to chase her this morning. We had a hard time keeping her out of your room."

"Why?"

He led her out into the tunnel and in the direction of 5th and Nightland.

"You're her hero, Nola," Kieran said, stopping and turning to face Nola so quickly she ran into him. "Literally. You saved her life." He ran a finger over her cheek. "You are braver than even I imagined." He turned and continued walking down the hall. "And now you've come to save all of us."

"The Outer Guard," Nola said as Kieran pushed through a heavy metal door and into a narrower tunnel. The low ceiling left only a few inches of clearance over Kieran's head. "Emanuel may think they can't get into Nightland, but they could. They're..." She searched for a less cowardly word than *terrifying*. "You know them. They aren't like everyone else in the domes. If they decide to come in here, they won't stop because they're destroying your home."

"Or killing people," Kieran growled. "I know. *We* know. But they don't know us. And when they try to come after us, they'll see. This isn't their city. It's ours."

They walked in silence for a moment, the tunnel becoming narrower and the lights dimmer. Sweat beaded on Nola's palms, burning the raw skin. She could feel the anger radiating from Kieran, overpowering her panic at being in the tunnel. He stopped at a dead end. Crumbling concrete and dirt had caved in the wall in front of them.

"What happened?" Nola asked. "Did a cave-in cover the garden?"

"We found our own way up." Kieran pointed at the ceiling above him to a narrow hole and a thin metal ladder. "You first."

Nola reached above her head to the ladder, but this was more than climbing out her window or even up the vent. Her fingers only grazed the bottom of the first rung.

Kieran's hands closed around her waist, and he lifted her up over his head. Nola grabbed for the ladder, gasping. "Thanks." Her arms shook, and the skin on her palms stung as she began to climb.

With a ringing *thunk* that shook the ladder, she felt Kieran launch himself onto the bottom rung. She closed her eyes for a moment, taking a breath before continuing to climb. Soon, even the dim light from the tunnel had disappeared. Nola groped the air in front of her, feeling for each rung to pull herself up.

"How far up are we going?" she asked after a few minutes when her muscles burned in protest.

"About 124 rungs," Kieran answered.

"Was I supposed to be counting?" Nola puffed.

"Nope," Kieran said, adding slowly, "but you should start watching your head... now."

Nola froze, waiting for something to swoop out of the blackness at her face.

"Reach up," Kieran's voice drifted through the darkness.

Hesitantly, Nola reached one hand overhead. Cold, flat metal blocked the path above her. She pushed, and the metal lifted easily, letting in a flood of outside air and the faint glow of the moon through the haze of the city. Giving the door a heave, she flipped it open with a loud *clang*, then climbed out into the night and onto a roof high above the city.

Rows of plants stretched out in front of her. Scraps of every kind had been used to make raised beds for the garden. A row of beans was surrounded by planks of an old painted sign for *The Freshest Oxygen Bar in Town*. An apple tree grew in the broken bed of a truck. Rows of melons sprouted from the base of an old shipping container.

"How?" Nola breathed, running her fingers along the leaves of a plant. The texture was perfect. No damage from the acid rain, no signs of blight.

"It takes a lot." Kieran leapt onto the edge of the old truck and pulled a red apple down from the tree. "We had to get miles away to find soil that wasn't contaminated by the old factories. It took a few months to find the right spot. By then, we had found enough planting containers, though getting them up here was a chore. We had to make sure none of the Outer Guard saw us hauling old truck beds up the side of the building."

"But they could have helped." Nola leaned in close to the apple tree and smelled the earth. The scent was different from the dirt in the domes, less pungent in its fertility, but still clean and fruitful. Free from the chemicals that flowed through the river.

"I don't think they want to help vampires." Kieran tossed the apple to Nola. "Even if the vampires are growing food for starving kids."

Nola ran her thumb along the smooth red skin of the apple. "But the forest, the trees there are dying from the rain. The chemicals burn them."

"These plants aren't watered with rain. Stay here." Kieran ran down the rows of strange planters.

Nola held the apple up to the moonlight. The fruit didn't match the size of those grown inside the glass, and the skin lacked the luscious, vibrant color expected of Lenora Kent's crops. It couldn't match the perfection of the domes.

This food can still save people's lives.

Nola looked out over the city. Only one building stood taller than the garden, blocking the light of the domes from view as though her home didn't exist at all.

The *buzz* of a rope being pulled quickly came from the direction where Kieran had disappeared. An odd flapping sound pounded all around the roof as long sheets of fabric unfurled from the sides of the plant beds. Hung from wires so dark Nola hadn't noticed them before, the cloth rose up high, floating into the sky like sails before, with a shuddering *whine*, they all turned at once, making a patchwork of fabric that covered the whole roof.

Before Nola could really begin to think through what she had just seen, Kieran had returned to her side.

Nola moved her mouth for a moment, searching for the right words.

"I designed it." Kieran beamed. "It took Desmond and Bryant a long time to find the material, but it works."

"How?" Nola gaped.

"The material is waterproof and coated against the rain. It's what the old triage tents were made of, back when there were doctors on the outside. They scavenged all of this, and then we built the pulley system. We put the fabric up to keep off the midday sun and any rain, but the rest of the time, we leave it open."

"But the water?" Nola climbed up onto the truck bed to feel the fabric. It was light and thin, but coated in something that felt rubbery, like the Outer Guard's jackets.

"The rain runs off of the tent and into a filtration system." Kieran shoved his hands into his pockets, looking every bit the proud genius Nola had known him to be. "It's rudimentary, but it gets the water for Nightland and for the plants clean enough to be used. And this is just one rooftop. If we could find the materials to farm on other roofs, we could feed the city. And if we could take all this with us, we could build a home somewhere without the smog of the factories and the stink from the river." Kieran grabbed Nola around the waist, sweeping her into his arms. "We could help people, really help them."

His dark eyes stared into hers, his gaze so intense she flushed and looked away.

"It's brilliant." Nola tucked her hair behind her ears and took a step away from Kieran.

"And it's all because of you," Kieran said. "All that studying in botanicals your mother was always making you do. It gave me the idea. I came up with the plan and built the pulley system. My dad did the chemical testing and pretty much everyone else in Nightland helped with the rest."

"And the guards never noticed?"

"We're still here." Kieran shrugged. He lifted Nola's hand that held the apple up in front of her. "Take a bite."

Carefully, Nola bit into the apple. Her teeth pierced the skin, and juice flowed into her mouth. Through the bitter metal tinge of the ReVamp, she could taste the sweetness of the fruit. "It's amazing," she whispered. "It's real food."

Kieran smiled. "I know."

Nola held out the apple for Kieran to take a bite.

"No, it's for you." Kieran shook his head, his gaze fixed on the juice dripping onto Nola's finger.

"But it's wonderful." Nola took a step toward him. "You should enjoy the fruits of your labor."

"No." The light of the moon caught the corner of his eyes. No color broke through the shadows. Only black where emerald green should have been.

Pain ripped through Nola's chest as the apple tumbled from her hand. "Kieran, you're a vampire."

CHAPTER NINETEEN

"Nola," Kieran said, reaching toward her.

Nola took a step back. Pain shot through her leg as something sharp cut into her calf. She didn't dare look away from Kieran as warm blood trickled down her ankle.

"Nola, you're hurt." Kieran stepped forward.

"Don't touch me." Nola felt for the truck bed behind her. She stepped sideways, gasping in pain as she put weight on her leg.

"Let me help you." Pain flooded Kieran's eyes. "Nola, I would never hurt you."

"You're a vampire," Nola spat.

"So, is Emanuel—"

"That's different."

"And Raina, and Desmond. You came out here to save vampires."

"But not you!" Nola shouted. "You weren't supposed to be like them." Tears streamed down her face.

"Why?" Kieran asked. "Why does it matter?"

"You drink blood?" Nola's voice quaked.

"Yes."

Nola choked on a sob.

"But not human blood, never human blood." Kieran took a step forward.

Nola tried to run, but her leg gave out under her, sending her tumbling to her knees.

"Nola," Kieran whispered.

She could hear his heart breaking as he said her name.

"I've never attacked a human," he said, his voice cold and dead. "I only drink animal blood."

Images of Kieran sucking the life from a poor animal's neck seized Nola's mind.

"We have a farm for the animals," Kieran said. "It's no different from eating meat."

"Yes it is." Nola tried to stand, but her leg couldn't bear any weight. "I thought you were trying to save the vampires. Find a way to make them human."

"You can't go back," Kieran said. "Once you're a vampire, the change is permanent. Either inject the Vamp or die. It's a one-way trip, Nola."

Nola sobbed on the ground. Kieran's green eyes were gone.

I'll never see them again.

"I had no choice," Kieran said. "I was running out of time."

"What?"

"After three months out here, I got sick," Kieran said. "I had been giving out food, there was a cough going around. It didn't do anything that bad to most people. But I didn't have the same immunities. After a few days, I couldn't breathe. My dad didn't know what to do. He had been working on a new kind of Vamp. One that didn't change people's personalities. It wasn't ready, but he didn't have a choice. I was drowning. Drowning in my own body. I was terrified. I was dying."

He knelt next to Nola, and she didn't back away.

"He gave me a small injection of ReVamp like he did for you, trying to get the disease out of me, but it didn't work. He had to give me a full dose. It felt like my lungs were on fire. I thought I would boil in my own skin. Then my lungs filled with ice. And then my whole body was filled with ice. I was sure I would freeze to death. But eventually, I stopped shaking, and I got used to the cold. It took a few days, but I woke up." Kieran looked into Nola's eyes. "I'm the first of the new vampires."

Nola looked down at Kieran's hand in hers. She hadn't realized she had reached for him. His cold skin sent chills up her arm.

"Does it feel different? Touching me?" Nola said.

"I can feel the blood flowing through your veins like lava," Kieran said. "But the heat doesn't hurt."

"They said in the domes that vampires hunt people, that they attack them and drink their blood."

"The ones on the streets do," Kieran said. "But not in Nightland. They only take blood they pay for."

"Pay for?"

"There are desperate people in the city," Kieran said. "They sell their blood to vampires. But most of us take the blood from the farm animals."

"So, even though—" Nola glanced down at her bloody leg, her wanting to know warring with her fear of Kieran.

"I can smell your blood," Kieran said before she could speak. "It smells sweet."

"I smell like candy?"

"A little. But I'm still me. And you know me, Nola. You know I would never hurt you. I would do anything to protect you."

Nola nodded, not trusting her voice.

Kieran placed his hand on Nola's cheek. A tingle ran down her spine, leaving goose bumps in its wake.

"We should get you back to my dad," Kieran said. "I think you need stitches."

"I don't know about that ladder," Nola said. "I can't even walk."

"Do you trust me?" Kieran grinned mischievously.

He looked like the old Kieran. Her Kieran, who she knew better than anyone, planning something that would scare and excite her. The Kieran who had taught her to climb onto her roof. The Kieran who would save a city with a garden.

"Absolutely."

In one swift movement, Kieran lifted Nola onto his back. "Hold on tight." He ran to the open trap door.

"You can't carry me all the way down," Nola said as Kieran twisted onto the ladder, taking two steps down and shutting them into the darkness.

"Just trust me, Nola," Kieran said before taking both hands off the ladder and launching them into the void.

The air rushing past them stole the scream from Nola's throat. Kieran laughed as they sped through the darkness.

Nola tightened her grip, holding onto Kieran with every bit of strength she had. And just when she began to fear the ground, Kieran landed as light as a cat on the tunnel floor.

Gently, he pried Nola's arms from his neck, pulling her around to cradle her as though she weighed nothing.

"I told you to trust me." Kieran smiled.

"Mmmmhmmm," was the only noise Nola could manage as she pulled herself closer to Kieran's chest.

Kieran pressed his cheek to her hair, rocking her gently for a moment.

"I didn't mean to scare you," he said.

"Of course you did. You always liked to scare me." Nola let go of his neck and smacked him on the chest. "But I'm not mad. It's nice to know—" Nola paused for a moment, searching for the right words. His heartbeat pounded through his chest and into her hand. Its rhythm beat slower than hers, pumping the cold blood through his body in a rhythm she didn't recognize. "It's nice to know your sense of humor hasn't changed."

Kieran beamed down at her. "Never. I'm still me, Nola. Just me with super strength... and a different appetite."

His smile disappeared, and his eyes begged her to understand.

"You're Kieran," Nola said. "You're still my Kieran."

He leaned down and brushed his lips against hers. The cold of his touch tingled her skin.

"I will always be yours," he whispered.

A door rasped open down the hall. Kieran cursed under his breath. "We need to get you back to my dad."

"It's not bleeding that badly." She didn't want to go back to the others. Back to the worn hospital gown and cold tools. If she could just stay here with Kieran for a few minutes.

"It's bad enough." Kieran walked down the tunnel.

Nola felt his muscles tensing as though he were preparing for a fight.

"I don't want to freak you out, but the other vampires will scent your blood."

"Scent my blood?" Nola looked down at her red-stained leg.

"You smell like fresh baked brownies," Kieran said, his voice tight.

"Do you need to leave me here?" Nola's voice came out as a squeak.

"I told you before, I would never bite a human." Kieran rounded the corner.

A dark shape waited for them in front of the door to the main corridor.

"But some of our people are recovering human biters," Kieran said. "We don't want them to relapse."

"What happened to her?" a deep voice called from the shadow.

"Cut her leg," Kieran said, his voice steady and calming as though he were trying to soothe a frightened animal. "I'm taking her up to my father now." Kieran took a step forward. "You know my father. Dr. Wynne."

"ReVamp." The man leaned out of the shadows. The scars covering his face twisted as he frowned. "He made ReVamp."

"Yes," Kieran said. "Have you had ReVamp?"

"I turned long before the good doctor decided to save us all." The long white scars cut through his skin as though something had clawed his face over and over again.

"Then you are one of the strongest to have joined Nightland," Kieran said, still walking forward. "It takes a special vampire to understand how we must change to survive."

"I did change to survive." The man tossed his bald head back, displaying more scars coating his neck. "I changed because my lungs were rotting. I came down here to be safe from the Outer Guard."

"Nightland is about more than being safe from the guards," Kieran said. "Nightland is about hope. It's about creating a better future."

"Nightland is about rules." The man took a step forward. "It's about protecting one man's vision while the rest of us hide underground."

"We aren't hiding," Kieran said.

Nola clung tighter to Kieran's neck as he shifted her weight in his arms.

"Every night we are working to make things better," Kieran said.

"Better for the ones who haven't been turned."

"Better for all of us." Kieran had stopped moving forward.

"Then why won't you let us eat?" the man roared.

Nola flew from Kieran's arms, landing on the ground behind him, knocking the wind from her. The thumping of fists on flesh came from behind her. The sharp crack of breaking bones and muffled yells echoed through the tunnel. Pain shot through her as she gasped, forcing air back into her lungs.

She rolled onto her side, trying to see who had been hit, but they were moving too quickly for her to know if either was hurt.

The man lifted Kieran, tossing him into the wall with a sickening *crunch*. Dust from the ceiling fell into Nola's eyes as the walls trembled.

The man took Kieran's head, slamming it back into the wall.

"No!" Nola screamed.

The man turned to her. His eyes were pitch black. He opened his mouth, hissing and showing two long, bright white fangs.

CHAPTER TWENTY

The vampire ran his tongue along the sharp tip of his left fang, coloring its point with his own blood.

Nola watched in horror as the vampire's blood dripped down his chin, making him look more animal than human.

"Leave her alone." Kieran launched himself onto the man's neck, sending him face first into the dirt. He grabbed the man's head, slamming it into the ground again and again until the man's screams of rage stopped.

Kieran let go of the man, standing up and jumping over the blood pooling on the dirt floor.

He reached down to Nola. Red coated his palms.

Nola tried to reach for him, but she couldn't make her arms move. The crimson pool seeped toward her.

"Nola," Kieran whispered. "He was going to kill you."

The man's bloody fangs flashed through Nola's mind as tears ran down her cheeks.

"He'll wake up in a few hours," Kieran said. "But I'll make sure Raina's found him before then."

"He's dead." Nola's voice cracked.

"He's a vampire. He'll heal. But I won't let him hurt you. Not ever." Kieran reached down for Nola again. "Can I touch you?"

Nola nodded, clinging to Kieran as soon as she was in his arms. She buried her face in his chest, squeezing her eyes shut as Kieran leapt over the man's body. She could feel the uneven pounding of the floor under Kieran's feet and the air flying past them and knew he was running. She wanted to look, to watch the tunnels fly by, seeing them as Kieran did. But she kept her eyes closed, afraid if she opened them, another pair of bloody fangs would be waiting.

Soon, Kieran slowed to a walk.

A door *clicked* open in front of them.

"What happened?" a voice with a lilting accent said.

Nola opened her eyes, and Julian was staring at her, his face tense. They were in the gallery. Julian held an open book in his hand.

"She cut her leg in the garden," Kieran said, not stopping his stride as Julian joined them. "I was trying to get her back here, and we were attacked."

"Someone thought she was a dinner bell, eh?" Julian said. "Did you kill them?"

Kieran shook his head. "Just smashed his head in. He'll wake up in a bit. He's in the last tunnel on the way to the garden."

"I'll get Raina." Julian held open the door to Emanuel's home before leaving them and walking back out through the gallery.

"What's Raina going to do to him?" Nola asked.

"Nothing more than he deserves," Kieran said.

The old woman in the kitchen looked up as they passed but didn't try to follow.

"What's going to happen?" Panic clenched Nola's chest.

"Raina will execute him," Kieran said. "We all make the deal when we choose to live in Nightland. No violence within these walls. No attacking humans. No attacking each other. That man is a monster. We can't keep him here. We can't let him out in the world, or he'll leave a string of bodies behind him, and we can't give him to the Outer Guard—"

"Or he'll tell them exactly where to find us," Nola said as Kieran swung open the door to Dr. Wynne's lab.

"What on Earth?" Dr. Wynne said, pushing up his glasses as he stared at Nola. "Was she stabbed again?"

"No, she cut her leg." Kieran lay Nola down on the cold metal table. "The apple tree truck."

"And your hand," Dr. Wynne said, glancing at Kieran as he cut away the bottom of Nola's pants, exposing the jagged gash.

Nola's stomach turned at the sight of her own ragged flesh.

"Broken," Kieran said. "Foot, too."

"What?" Nola tried to sit up on the table to look at Kieran, but he grabbed her shoulder, holding her down.

"Do you need it set?" Dr. Wynne asked, seemingly unconcerned by his son's broken bones.

Kieran flexed his hand and stomped his foot a few times. "Just the hand."

"Pardon me, Nola," Dr. Wynne said, disappearing behind Nola's head. There was silence for a moment, and then a sharp *crack* and a muffled groan.

"Thanks," Kieran said, coming around to Nola's side, keeping his right hand by his chest and gripping Nola's hand with the left.

"Are you all right?" Nola asked.

Dr. Wynne fluttered around the laboratory, gathering tools.

"Fine." Kieran smiled down at Nola, only the corners of his eyes betraying any pain. "It'll be healed in an hour or so. One of the vampire perks."

"Speaking of vampire perks," Dr. Wynne said, placing a tray of tools next to Nola, "I'm afraid your food is going to be distasteful for longer than anticipated. I can stitch you back together, but you've lost a fair bit of blood, and with the rust and filth on that truck bed, the risk for infection is too significant. I'm going to stitch you back together and give you another localized dose of ReVamp."

Dr. Wynne raised a hand as Kieran began to protest. "She will be at no risk of being changed, but I don't think her mother would like her returned to the domes sans a leg."

"You're sure it won't change her?" Kieran asked. "Dad, you have to be sure."

"I am quite sure." Dr. Wynne picked up a threaded needle. "ReVamp will only affect the brain and circulatory system if it is injected directly into the blood stream. Think of this as a localized anesthetic."

Kieran opened his mouth to argue again, but Dr. Wynne waved him away. "You must trust me, Kieran. I did invent the stuff after all." He turned to Nola. "You might want to take a deep breath, dear, I have nothing to numb you with."

Nola squeezed Kieran's hand, shutting her eyes tight as the needle pierced her leg.

Her stomach seized at the tugging of the thread pulling through her skin.

"Prison," Nola said through gritted teeth, searching for something to distract her from the nauseating sensation of her flesh being violated by a needle and thread. "The man who attacked us, why can't he go to vampire prison?"

"There's no such thing as vampire prison," Kieran said with a touch of laughter in his voice.

The needle pierced Nola's leg again, and she redoubled her grip on Kieran's hand. "But we're underground. With all the tunnels, why can't you make a prison? Then you could lock him up instead of just killing him."

"We barely have the resources to keep Nightland safe from the outside," Dr. Wynne said, his voice low and slow as he continued to work on Nola's leg. "And if the Outer Guard really are going to try to break in, well, we can't afford to have people guarding someone who attempted to kill a Nightland guest."

"Put him in a steel room and deliver him meals," Nola said, trying hard not to think of the fact that *she* had nearly been the vampire's meal.

"He's a vampire, Nola," Kieran said, stroking her hair as she bit her lip, trying not to pull away from the pain.

There was the *tink* of metal on metal and the sound of footsteps walking away.

"If we left him alone, he could try and dig his way out or tear through the stone," Kieran said. "There aren't many things an angry vampire can't break through given enough time. And we only have enough of that kind of metal for the door to the outside. There isn't a way for us to lock him up."

"Silver doors all around?" Nola said.

Kieran chuckled. "Vampires can touch silver."

"So, it's not like the sun allergy *going to get lots of blisters and die* type thing?" Nola asked as Dr. Wynne's footsteps returned.

"Well," Dr. Wynne said, "I wouldn't recommend wearing silver as some irritation can occur. A bit of discoloration and some nasty swelling in rare cases, but if you're afraid of a vampire, I wouldn't suggest trying to kill them with a silver cross. It could take hours for him to be bothered with it at all. This will sting a bit."

A needle pierced Nola's skin again. Pure ice poured into her flesh, freezing the wound on her leg. Nola groaned as cold unlike anything she'd ever felt before seared her skin.

Keep breathing. You have to keep breathing.

Opening her eyes, she glanced down at her leg. The skin around the wound had become stark white, while the cut itself turned a violent red.

"Don't watch it," Kieran said, taking Nola's face in his hands and turning her to look into his eyes. "It's better if you don't watch it."

Nola let out a deep, shuddering breath. "What about stakes through the heart? Is that true? Should there be a ban on wood in Nightland?"

"If you destroy a vampire's heart, he will die," Dr. Wynne said.

The sound of metal instruments being laid on a metal tray came from the end of the table, but Nola didn't look away from Kieran.

The ice in her leg had changed now, from something stagnant to something squirming as though worms crawled under her skin.

"It's about the only thing a vampire can't heal from," Dr. Wynne continued. "Well that," he paused, "and decapitation. But I see hardly any of that in here. It is very hard to cut an entire head off without meaning to. And if you meant to cut a person's head off, I don't know why you'd bother bringing them to me for help. At that point, it's really a matter of hiding the body where it won't smell too terribly and the Outer Guard won't find it. I suppose that's what makes the river so popular for those things. But there must be lots of other choices—"

"Thanks, Dad." Kieran cut his father off just as Nola began to wonder how many bodies had been dumped in the river and if there were any bones left or if the toxicity was so high everything had been eaten away.

"You can sit up now," Dr. Wynne said, pushing himself backwards on his rolling stool.

Nola opened her eyes a crack to look at her leg. The squirming had stopped. Now it felt like someone was holding a bag of particularly cold ice on her calf. The skin around the cut was still pale, but the cut itself was what made Nola sit up to examine her leg more closely.

There were twelve stitches in her leg, holding together a cut that looked to be at least a few days old. Shiny new skin had bridged the gap between the two ragged sides.

"The stitches will make sure everything heals in the right place, and the scarring should be minimal," Dr. Wynne said, his brow furrowed and lips pinched as though afraid Nola might not approve of his handiwork.

"That's incredible." Nola poked the cut before Kieran lifted her hand away. "If they had this in the domes—"

"They'd never use it," Dr. Wynne said. "ReVamp alters you at a genetic level. Not badly for you. In a week, you won't notice you were ever injected. Still, the whole point of the domes is to preserve a genetically healthy human race. ReVamp changes the way DNA works. It alters your body at the most basic level. Why do you think they despise the vampires so much?"

"Because all the ones they deal with are violent." Nola's voice rose in excitement. "If you could show them this—"

"Then they'd still kill us all if they had the chance," Raina said as she slunk into the room. "A drug is a drug, impure genes are impure genes, and a vampire is a vampire. They don't see differences. It's all black and white, and they don't give a shit how many of us die out here."

Nola opened her mouth to argue, but Raina held up a finger.

"Please don't fight me on things you don't understand, little girl. You'll make me sorry I didn't manage to stab you through the heart."

"You're the one that stabbed me?" Nola said, looking at the knife tucked into Raina's belt.

Raina followed her gaze. "Did you expect me to throw my knife away in remorse? You were sneaking around."

Nola opened her mouth to explain, but Raina cut her off with the wave of a hand.

"I know you were coming to save us from the big, bad guards. And I do appreciate the sentiment. But the way I see it, it wasn't my fault you were in a very bad place at the wrong time, and I did lend you some of my very fine old clothes. And since you'll apparently be needing to borrow yet another pair of pants, as you can't seem to keep from bleeding all over the place even if I didn't cause it, I would say we're pretty even."

"Pants versus stab wound," Kieran said, one dark eyebrow raised. "That's a rough trade to call."

"It's a cold, cruel world. You take what you can get." Raina glared at Nola. "We're good, right?"

Nola nodded. "We're good."

"Excellent." Raina flashed a smile that made Nola more nervous than the knife had. "Because we've figured out a way to get you home. And any trust issues could definitely get a few people killed."

Nola looked to Kieran who gave the slightest shrug.

"Emanuel wants us all to meet in the gallery." Raina turned back toward the door.

"It must be a grand plan if he wants us in the gallery," Dr. Wynne said, moving over to a sink in the corner to wash his hands. "He always likes to make big announcements in there."

Kieran took Nola's hand and helped her off the table. Her leg still felt shaky as she put pressure on it, but the unbearable pain and terrible weakness had gone.

"Thank you, Dr. Wynne," she said, taking his hand in hers as he moved for the door. His skin was warm to the touch.

"Of course, dear." Dr. Wynne smiled. "You are family. And, well, it is my job, I suppose."

"I'll help her." Kieran wrapped an arm around Nola's waist. "You go on ahead."

"Your dad," Nola whispered as soon as Dr. Wynne was in the hall, "he hasn't taken ReVamp, has he?"

"No. He hasn't needed it yet. He had more immunities than I did from sneaking in and out so much, and he doesn't think people should take it unless they have no other choice. How did you know?"

"His hands are still warm," Nola said, sinking into the cold of Kieran's hand cutting through the leather that separated their skin. "And his eyes are still green, like yours used to be."

"Very observant," Kieran said as they walked into the hall, him supporting most of Nola's weight. "He'll have to take it soon, though."

"What wrong with him?"

"He's started losing weight. He can't focus. He goes on tangents even worse than usual."

"Maybe being underground is getting to him," Nola said. "Maybe, if he got out—"

"He's too valuable," Kieran said. "They won't let him go where they can't protect him."

"Even if he wants to?" Nola stopped walking and nearly toppled over as Kieran continued forward.

"This is about saving people, thousands of people. He understands that," Kieran said. "He's starting to show signs of toxicity poisoning. If he takes ReVamp, he'll get better. And when we get out of Nightland, he'll get all the fresh air he wants."

Kieran pushed through the heavy, wooden door into the gallery.

Bryant and Desmond sat stone-faced on one of the large couches. Raina sat next to Dr. Wynne while Julian leaned on a bookshelf, and all of their eyes were fixed on Emanuel who stood in the center of it all.

"Nola." Emanuel spread his arms to her. "I see you've recovered nicely from your accident."

"Yes," Nola said, suddenly aware that everyone's attention had shifted to her. "Dr. Wynne is brilliant, and the garden was amazing."

"I'm glad you appreciate what we are trying to accomplish here"—Emanuel's brief smile vanished—"as I am afraid we need to ask for your help once again."

CHAPTER TWENTY-ONE

"What kind of help?" Nola asked, resisting as Kieran tried to guide her to a chair.

Emanuel paced across the carpet. "The only way to get you home is for the domes to believe you were brought here against your will. If we are operating under the guise that vampires broke into the domes and kidnapped you, then, and I mean no offense, we must also maintain that we wish to give you back. I am sure we can all agree it would be a very unlikely story that we in Nightland kidnapped sweet Nola and she managed to escape us and arrive home undamaged."

The group in the room nodded.

After a reluctant moment, Nola nodded, too. "I don't think I could escape a few hundred vampires in an underground lair alive."

"Good." Emanuel's shoulders relaxed. "We've contacted the domes and informed them of your kidnapping and made our ransom demand."

"What did you ask for?" Nola's said.

If the domes have to give something vital, it could put the whole system in danger. The life boat could sink, and it would be my fault.

"We asked for things that will be very valuable to us and can be easily replaced by the domes," Emanuel said. "Common seeds of plants that no longer grow on the outside. A few doses of medicine for the children. Nothing the domes will even miss."

Nola nodded.

"We've asked them to meet us on the bridge tomorrow, an hour before dawn," Emanuel continued. "That should make them feel secure while giving us ample time to get back underground. By daybreak, you'll be cozy in the domes, and Kieran will have some new seeds for the garden."

"But if they think you broke in and kidnapped me, won't that give the Outer Guard a reason to come after you?" Nola asked.

"They don't need a reason to come after us," Desmond said. "They'll come no matter what we do."

"And you have to be back in the domes when the Outer Guard bang on our door." Raina's hand rested on the hilt of her knife as though expecting the Outer Guard to run into the gallery as they spoke.

Nola reached for Kieran's hand. "But what will I tell them when they ask me what happened?"

"That's where I come in," Julian said. "We've worked it all out so you can give them enough details to be believable without telling them anything that could endanger Nightland. I'll coach you on all of it. Dr. Wynne and Kieran won't be involved. As far as the Outer Guard will know, we broke through the glass in Bright Dome to get you."

"They'll seal it," Nola said. The squirming knot of fear in her stomach disappeared, leaving her hollow. "I won't be able to get back out."

"I think," Dr. Wynne said, looking down at his hands, "that will probably be for the best."

"You almost died out here, Nola," Kieran said, turning to face her. "Next time, you might not make it through the woods."

"So, I'll just never see you again?" Nola's voice was tight, higher than usual. "I'll just go back to the domes—"

"And live the life you're meant to have," Dr. Wynne said. "You can't keep going back and forth, and you can't stay out here."

"Why?" Tears crept into Nola's eyes. "Why can't I stay? You need me. I could help with the garden. I know more about agriculture than any of you."

"You'd get sick," Kieran said, his voice barely a whisper as he brushed the tears from Nola's cheek. "You'd get hurt. I won't let you die out here."

"What about ReVamp?" Nola said, remembering the bitter taste of metal in her mouth. "It saved you."

"You could never go home." Pain filled Kieran's eyes. "You would never see your mother again. I want to keep you more than anything, but I won't take the sun away from you, Nola."

He pulled Nola into his arms, and she buried her face in his shoulder. "How many times are we going to have to say goodbye?"

"Not to be completely insensitive," Raina said, "but a few of us still have to risk our lives to get the princess back to the castle. So, rather than focus on true love lost to circumstance and the bad luck of her going back to Jeremy my-father-wants-to-destroy-Nightland for comfort—"

"Raina, don't," Kieran muttered.

"Don't tell the truth? I think we all know why Jeremy gave Nola the info that sent her here. And we can be sure the Domer will take care of her once we make the trade."

Nola's cheeks flushed in anger and embarrassment.

"Let's stop pretending this is *Romeo and Juliet* unless you both want to end up dead. Why don't we give Nola to Julian to make sure she doesn't get herself caught for being a traitor, and once they're done, you two can go feel each other up in a dark corner."

The room froze for a long moment.

Bryant moved first. "Gonna go make sure we have enough vamps on board for the swap."

Desmond followed him out into the tunnels.

"I'll take you to the kitchen to work on your story," Julian said, awkwardly patting his hands on the sides of his legs. "I think we have something that resembles tea for you to drink."

"Anyone want to help me bury the guy who tried to kill Nola?" Raina asked, looking at Kieran.

"Just go, Raina," Kieran said, his face stony and impossible for Nola to read.

"All the dirty work for me. How kind." Raina stepped forward, baring her teeth.

Julian's hand closed around Nola's arm, and he led her from the gallery.

The door muffled Kieran's shouted response.

"Does it all make sense?" Julian asked as Nola finished her third cup of what was not really tea.

"Yes." Nola traced a jagged line that had been carved into the wooden kitchen table with her fingertip.

"It's about more than being able to repeat the details to me." Julian sipped from his dark mug.

Nola had closed her eyes when he had poured something from the refrigerator into it. *Knowing* he was probably drinking blood and actually *seeing* him do it were two very different things.

"You have to understand the story you're telling," Julian said.

"I get it." Nola kneaded the point of pain that pierced her forehead. "You kidnapped me to find out whatever you could about what my mother had learned at the Green Leaf Conference. I got hit on the head and stabbed a bit. Told you what you wanted to know since it didn't really matter anyway. You made the trade."

"Good girl." Julian tapped his knuckles on the table.

Nola dug her fingers into the wood, watching the white of her knuckles blossom through the red scars on her hands. "What if I don't want to?"

"Want to what?" Julian cocked his head to the side.

"What if I don't want you to make the trade?" Nola said. "What if I want to stay in Nightland? Help with your work."

"Kieran's already explained." Sympathy crept into Julian's voice. "If you stay here, you'll end up a vampire. Perhaps not right away, but eventually it would be either ReVamp or death."

"But being a vampire doesn't seem so bad."

"It's not," Julian said. "It took me a few years to get off the human blood and a decade more to forgive myself for all I'd done. But once you get used to blood and darkness, it's not such a bad life."

"Then let me stay," Nola said. "I want to be here. I want to help you save people."

I want to be with Kieran.

Julian studied his pale hands for a long moment. "I'm afraid that's impossible."

"But you just said—"

"I said being a vampire wasn't that bad. I didn't say you could be allowed to stay in Nightland."

"But—"

"They know you're here, Nola," Julian said. "We've told the domes we kidnapped you. If we don't give you back to them, it could start a war. And if the domes decided to fight the vampires in earnest, I don't even want to begin to imagine how terrible the damage to both sides would be. You have to go back. There is nothing else to be done."

"I could tell them it was me. That I ran away. Then they'll banish me."

"Think, Nola. Between the story we've written for you and the truth, which do you think they're most likely to believe?"

"But if I only tell them the truth, your story won't matter."

"They know the beginning of our kidnapping tale," Julian said.

"That will be enough. They'll claim brainwashing or coercion. We have to give you back in the trade. It's the only way."

"The only solution is a lie," Nola said.

"A lie, yes." Julian patted Nola's hand. "And a hope you might eventually forget how wonderful the truth you lost could have been."

Nola closed her eyes, hating the sympathy on Julian's face.

"We can work on your story again tonight," Julian said, taking Nola's cup to the sink. "It's late. You should get some sleep."

"By late you mean early?" Nola's head spun from fatigue and trying to keep everything straight in her mind. What had happened since she left the domes, what she had to say had happened, and what could never happen.

"The morning is rather new." Julian washed both of their cups.

"Do vampires sleep?"

"Yes." Julian gave a half-shrug. "Most sleep at least an hour or two a day, mostly out of habit. We can go for a week or more without really feeling the physical need to sleep. But when days don't end, it takes a toll on the mind."

A door in the back of the kitchen opened, and a tiny girl emerged, her curly hair still rumpled from sleep.

"Eden." Julian swept the little girl into his arms.

Eden's face split into a grin, and she giggled as Julian rocked her back and forth.

"How are you this fine morning?" Julian said.

Eden bit her lips together, her brown eyes on Nola.

"Don't be afraid," Julian said, following Eden's gaze. "You know Nola. She's the one who got you your medicine. Can you say *thank you, Nola?*"

"Thank you, Nola," Eden said in a voice barely loud enough to be heard before burying her face in Julian's neck.

"Why don't we take Nola someplace she can get a bit of sleep, and then you and I can go find your father?" Julian asked.

Eden nodded.

Julian led Nola into the hallway and toward the room lined with bunks. Nola expected him to lead her to one of the metal bunk beds, but instead, he walked farther down the hall than Nola had been before.

"I'm sure no one will mind." Julian stopped at an unmarked door and gave it a cursory knock before swinging it open. "Sleep well."

Nola stepped into the room, not turning as the door closed behind her.

It was Kieran's room. She could tell without him even being there. He and his father had barely been able to take anything with them when they left the domes. A few pictures hung on the wall. Kieran with his parents all smiling at a party. Kieran and Nola high up in the willow tree in Bright Dome.

There were sketches of plants and animals. And Nola. She stared back at herself from the wall.

But the drawing was a perfected version of herself. The shape of the face was right, and so were the eyes. The pale freckles that dotted her nose and the tiny mark near her eye were all there. Still, she looked different. Calm, beautiful, and angelic.

A version of me I could never hope to be.

Nola reached up for the picture, wanting to study it, to see what Kieran's idea of her could teach her, but the door opened again.

"Julian said he was done for the morning," Kieran said, glancing from Nola to the sketch of 'perfect Nola.'

Heat rose in Nola's cheeks. "We're done."

"Sorry," Kieran said, running a hand through his hair, "if that's weird." He swept a hand toward the sketch. "You weren't supposed to see that."

"It's beautiful," Nola said.

"Not as beautiful as the original."

His words hung in the air for a moment.

"I haven't seen you draw anything since—" Nola paused.

Why am I making this worse?

"Since my mom died." Kieran picked up a pad of paper from the desk. His mother's face gazed up at them, a smile caught on her lips. "It took a while."

Nola took Kieran's hand, squeezing it tightly.

"You should get some sleep." Kieran lifted a small pile of clothes from the bed and tossed it onto the ground.

Nola laughed.

"I know," Kieran said. "Even down here where I hardly own anything I still can't keep my room clean. Dad comes in here every day to stare at the mess."

"Some things don't change."

"Maybe," Kieran said, his eyes locking with Nola's for a moment before flicking away.

"Kieran, Jeremy and I," Nola said, willing herself to get the words out before she lost her chance, "we're not together."

"Yet."

"No."

"You've kissed him," Kieran said. It wasn't a question. "You've kissed him. And even if you're not together yet, even if you're not in love with him yet, you will be."

"No, I won't."

"He's a good guy, Nola." Pain etched Kieran's words. "Hell, he's probably a better guy than I ever could have been even if I'd stayed in the domes. He's steady and strong. When you get home, he'll take care of you. He'll be with you every day while you try to forget what you saw down here. And then one day you'll realize he's the best thing you've got. And in a few years the Marriage Board will tell you it's time to pick someone as your pair, and you'll pick him. You'll get married, have kids, and forget all about Nightland—"

Nola cut off his words with a smack. Her hand throbbed from hitting Kieran's face, but she couldn't see more than his blurred outline through her tears.

"How dare you," Nola said. "How dare you decide what my life will be, what Jeremy's life will be?"

"I didn't decide. The domes did."

"What if that's not what I want?" Nola yelled. "I don't want to be with Jeremy just because—"

"Because it's the way things work for Domers."

"Because I can't have you." Nola sank down to her knees. "You say I have to go back to the domes to survive, but what kind of life will I have?"

Kieran knelt, wrapping his arms around her. He smelled like he always had, the scent she had known for years.

Are vampires supposed to smell so human?

"That's the problem with trying to save the human race," Kieran whispered. "You lose humanity."

Nola swiped her tears away with trembling hands.

Kieran lifted her onto the bed. "Sleep, Nola."

Nola shook her head as more tears streamed down her face. "I can't. If this is it, if I never get to see you again, I want to be with you. I don't want to sleep. I don't want to miss it."

"You aren't going to miss anything," Kieran murmured. "I'll be right here. I'll hold you close. And when you wake up, you'll still be in my arms. Won't that be a thing to remember?"

He lay down next to Nola, and she put her head on his shoulder in the place where she fit so perfectly.

"Goodnight, Nola," Kieran whispered. "I love you."

His words ran through her, filling her up before shattering her.

"I love you, too."

CHAPTER TWENTY-TWO

Ice surrounded her. But something deep in the back of her mind told her to hold the ice closer even as she shivered. That the cold she was feeling was precious and not to be let go.

"Nola," a voice whispered as the cold began to move away. "Nola, you're shaking." Lips brushed her forehead.

Nola's eyes fluttered open, and Kieran was gazing down at her. She pulled herself closer to his chest, not looking away from his eyes. Their black was still rimmed in a thin band of gold-speckled green.

"I don't mind the cold." Nola traced her fingers along Kieran's chin. A strong chin. A man's chin. Bits of stubble caught on her fingers.

When did we become grownups? Did it happen before the world got this dark or after?

Kieran wrapped both arms around her, pulling her to his chest. Nola closed her eyes, relishing the feeling of being held so tight he could not possibly let go.

"It's time to get up anyway," Kieran said, again pressing his lips to her forehead. "Bea will have breakfast waiting for you, and Julian will want to talk through your story again."

"Can't they wait?" Nola gripped Kieran's t-shirt with her fingers.

"Probably not."

Nola's stomach squirmed at the regret in his voice.

"How long before it's time?"

"Eight hours until you leave Nightland. Nine until the exchange."

Nola's ribcage turned to stone. She couldn't breathe. Her lungs had no space to expand. "That's not much time."

"Let's not waste any of it." Kieran tipped Nola's chin up. Softly, gently, he kissed her.

Nola's heart raced. She pressed herself against him, memorizing the feeling of his body next to hers.

With a creak, the bedroom door swung open.

Nola gasped as Dr. Wynne stared down at them, his face a mix between confusion and disappointment.

"Nola, you're needed in the kitchen." Dr. Wynne's voice was brusque and businesslike, something Nola had rarely heard from him.

Nola awkwardly struggled to climb over Kieran without looking him or Dr. Wynne in the face.

The bed springs creaked as Kieran stood.

"Nola, to the kitchen," Dr. Wynne said. "Kieran, stay here."

Nola walked out into the hall without looking back.

The door slammed behind her. She squeezed her eyes shut and took a shuddering breath.

They'll let me say goodbye to Kieran.

They would have to or...

Or what?

She would refuse to go back to the domes in the exchange and let the Outer Guard destroy Nightland?

A laugh shook Nola's chest. A high hysterical laugh she wouldn't have recognized as her own if she hadn't felt it ripping from her throat.

"I like it." Raina's voice pulled Nola from her frenzy. "A little insanity. It'll help sell the kidnapping story to the Domers."

"A *little* insanity perhaps." Julian peered over Raina's shoulder, his dark cup already in his hand. "But if she really has lost her mind, she might not be able to remember what to tell them, and then where would we be?"

"I remember," Nola said. "I remember all of it. I know the coat and trying to escape. I know I was dropped and there were lots of voices. I know all of it." Nola tugged a hand through her knotted hair. "I'm a quick learner. Just let me go back to Kieran."

"Really? You've already been in there all night," Raina said.

"And I'd really like for you to shut up!" Nola growled.

Raina smiled and tossed her purple and scarlet hair over her shoulder. "Is that what you want?"

"I think Raina should go back to practicing killing things," Julian said, stepping around Raina, "and Nola should come and brush up her details with me. Raina will get to stab things, which always makes her more cheerful, and the sooner Nola and I are done, the sooner she can be swept back into young love's tender throes."

"Fine." Raina turned and sauntered back toward to gallery. "See you in a few."

Julian gave Nola a tight smile. "After you."

The old woman was already standing over the stove in the kitchen, poking at something in a pan with a wooden spoon.

Nola sat down in the same seat she had taken the night before, willing herself not to start tracing the scratch with her finger again.

The *clink* of a plate being pulled from the cupboard brought Nola's attention back to the present as Bea shuffled over with breakfast—grilled vegetables and a little hunk of meat.

"Thank you," Nola murmured, deciding not to ask what sort of meat it was. She sniffed the plate, her mouth beginning to water. Carefully, she speared a green vegetable onto her fork. It tasted earthy and pungent, but like food.

"No more tinny taste?" Julian asked.

"It's gone," Nola said. She watched as Julian took a sip from his cup. "Do you miss food?"

"Me?" Julian chuckled. "No." He paused for a moment. "No, I really don't miss eating. But then, I was so ill before I became a vampire, eating had ceased to be a real option for me, so I suppose I am a terrible judge."

"Right."

"Now, down to business." Julian rubbed his hands together. "Who moved the glass?"

The next few hours passed slowly, Julian asking Nola the same questions in slightly different ways until her head spun.

"Well," Julian said when Nola had explained how she had gotten out of the Iron Dome for the twelfth time, "I think that's as good as we're going to get. And just remember, if you get confused, tell them you hit your head and all you remember is darkness and fear. Hopefully they'll feel sorry enough for you to leave you alone until you can sort out what you're supposed to say."

"You know the Outer Guard," Nola said as real fear clawed at her stomach. "They aren't known for their kindness and compassion."

"Careful, Nola," Julian said, "you're starting to sound like a Nightlander. I think our time here is done." Julian looked over Nola's shoulder.

Nola turned to find Kieran leaning against the doorframe. His dark hair stuck out at odd angles, and anger marked his face.

"I tried to keep things as swift as possible."

"Thanks, Julian," Kieran said, stepping into the kitchen and taking Nola's hand.

"Get our Cinderella back here by three. We don't want her to be late for the party being held in her honor." Julian nodded to them both and left the room, still holding his cup.

"How did it go?" Kieran asked after a long moment.

"Good," Nola said. "At least I think it went well. I've never been prepped to tell a giant lie before. What did your dad say?"

"Nothing." Kieran pressed his palm to his forehead. "Everything I already knew and had decided to forget. Dad's great at that."

Nola took Kieran's hands in her own, tracing the calluses that marked his palms with her finger.

"What do we do now?" Nola asked, studying Kieran's face, trying to memorize every line, even those formed by anger.

"If we were in the domes," Kieran said, twisting his hands so their fingers laced perfectly together, "I would say we should climb onto your roof and look at the stars."

"Or go lay under the willow tree," Nola said. "How many hours do you think we spent under that tree? Not talking or doing anything really. Just being together."

"Not nearly enough."

Nola laid her head on his shoulder. "We could go back to the garden."

"It's raining again," Kieran said. "Besides, I don't think Emanuel will let me take you aboveground until it's time. It's too risky."

"I can't just sit here." Nola stepped away from Kieran, her body telling her to run from the room. To keep running and running so the world couldn't catch her. "I can't just sit and count down the time. I need to do something."

"You've never been good at waiting." Kieran caught Nola around the waist, pulling her back into his arms.

"Never." Nola wound her arms around him. Her stomach purred.

If Dr. Wynne hadn't walked in, where would we be right now?

"I have an idea." Kieran swayed side to side with Nola as though they were dancing. "Let's go to Nightland."

"We're in Nightland." Nola laughed in spite of herself as Kieran twirled her under his arm.

"5th and Nightland. Let's go dance. We'll forget morning is ever coming."

Nola leaned in and kissed him. "Promise you'll hold me?"

"Until the sun comes up."

Kieran took her hand and led her out to the gallery.

Nola expected there to be someone at the door to make them stay in Emanuel's house, but Kieran led her into the tunnel without interruption. Whatever Dr. Wynne had said, he wasn't keeping Kieran from 5th and Nightland.

They didn't talk as they walked. What was there to say?

The closer they got to the club, the more Nola worried she wouldn't fit in with the other revelers.

I'm wearing Raina's old clothes. I can't get much more vampire than that without ReVamp.

Every few hundred yards, a vampire stood against the wall. They didn't wear any sort of uniform, but something about their posture, the way their gaze followed her and Kieran, made Nola certain they were guards.

"Did Emanuel put the extra guards on watch?" Nola whispered as they passed another guard, this one a boy not much older than herself with flaming red hair. "Because of the Outer Guard?" The red-haired boy's neck stiffened at the mention of the Outer Guard.

"Yes," Kieran said. "The housing tunnel is under strict watch. The club can defend itself, and so can the working areas. But this tunnel is where the kids are. The ones who can't fight. It's where Eden would be if Emanuel weren't her father."

The hairs on Nola's neck prickled at the thought of Eden hiding from the Outer Guard.

"Don't worry." Kieran kissed Nola's hand. "We're safe down

here. You warned us, and we're better protected than we have ever been before."

A thumping noise echoed in the distance. A low, rhythmic buzz that shook the floor under Nola's feet.

Nola's heart began to race as they grew closer to the music of Nightland. Two tall guards stood, arms crossed, knives in their belts, in front of the metal door.

One of them lifted his head as Nola approached as though sniffing the air.

"That her?" he said to Kieran who nodded.

The other guard turned and swung open the door. The music flooded into the hall so loudly Nola could barely hear herself call "thank you" as the guards ushered her past.

Flashes bounced down from the ceiling, throwing lights so bright into Nola's eyes, she was blinded when she tried to look into the shadows.

Vampires filled every corner of the club. The music thumped into her very bones. Each vibration shook her lungs, making it impossible for her to get a deep breath.

Kieran laced his fingers through hers, leading her out into the mass of surging bodies to find a place on the dance floor. Every time they passed a group of revelers, their eyes locked onto Nola.

"They're all staring at me," Nola whispered.

"Huh?" Kieran shouted above the music.

"They're all staring at me." Nola pressed her lips to Kieran's ear.

Kieran looked around the crowd, giving a nod to a group of vampires with dark red and black tattoos etched into their skin. "No one here will hurt you." He wrapped his arm around Nola's waist.

"Because they're all nice vampires who don't believe in eating Domers?" The question caught in Nola's throat.

"Because you're with me." Kieran smiled and swayed with the

music. "Because they know you're the Domer who came here to help us."

The people around them began to dance again, surging as one massive unit. Kieran held Nola tightly, swaying gently. "Ignore them," he said. "Let it just be us."

Nola looked into Kieran's eyes. The green was almost gone now, replaced with black. But the darkness didn't frighten her. In his eyes she could see his soul pouring out to her with every glance.

Kieran smiled and took her by the hand, spinning her under his arm. Nola tossed her head back and laughed. The music swallowed the sound of her laughter, but it didn't matter. Kieran was laughing with her. He pulled her back into his chest, one arm wrapped around her waist, holding her tight.

He brushed the loose hair from the sweat on her forehead. He ran his fingers over her curls as though hoping to memorize each strand. The music changed, and the crowd around them cheered. This song was faster, with shouted words Nola couldn't understand.

Kieran didn't sway with this song. He only gazed at Nola, sadness filling his eyes.

"Nola..." his mouth formed the word, but Nola couldn't hear the sound. She laced her fingers together around his neck, leaning up until their lips met.

She tightened her fingers in his hair, pulling him even closer. His heartbeat thudded through her chest, overpowering the music until there was nothing left but him. His hands traced the skin from her waist to her ribs. She gasped at the ice of his fingers.

Their eyes met for a moment before he was kissing her again, wrapping his arms around her so her feet left ground. She disappeared, lost in a haze. There was nothing left in the world but her and Kieran. Cheers and shouts glided past, but she cared for nothing except Kieran and her hunger for him. She teased his lips, reveling in his taste.

A loud *clang* shook the air, and Nola looked up. Her feet still hovered above the ground as Kieran held her, but they were in a tunnel away from the crowds of 5th and Nightland. The thick stone walls muffled the thumping of the music. Lamps dotted the corridor, leading off into the darkness, but no shapes moved in the shadows. They were alone.

CHAPTER TWENTY-THREE

"Nola," Kieran breathed, pressing his lips to hers gently at first, then with growing desperation.

This is it. All we'll ever have.

Kieran lifted her against the wall and pressed himself to her as his hands explored the bare skin of her back. Nola pulled herself closer to him, as though they could melt into one and the bridge would never come. She moaned as Kieran's fingers grazed her ribs, sending pulses of pleasure trembling through her.

"Kieran," she breathed, wrapping herself around him.

This is perfect. This is right.

"No." Kieran stepped away.

Nola crumpled to the ground, hitting her head on the stone wall.

"What?" Nola said, blinking to see Kieran past the stars that danced in front of her eyes.

"I want you, Nola," Kieran said, his voice desperate and sad. "I want to keep you here. I want to make you mine."

"Then do it." Nola swallowed the lump of fear in her throat as her words hung in the air. "I'm not afraid."

Kieran stepped forward, taking Nola's hands and helping her

to her feet. She swayed as pain shot through her head, but the ache did nothing to shadow the longing that filled her. Kieran traced her lips with his finger, then placed his hand over her heart.

"You have to get to the bridge." Kieran turned and walked down the tunnel.

"Kieran," Nola said, forcing her feet to move as she ran after him. "We have time."

"A few hours," Kieran said, not slowing his stride.

"One night. You said we could have one night. I thought—"

"I want you, Nola." Kieran turned to face her. He took both her arms, holding her tight. "More than anything, I want you. But the whole point in giving you back to the domes is to make sure you have a life."

"I can have a life tomorrow."

"And what would you tell Jeremy?" Kieran said. "Would you lie? Never mention it happened? Or would you admit you gave yourself to a Vamper in a filthy tunnel?"

"It's none of Jeremy's business."

"You belong with him!" Kieran pulled away from Nola and paced the tunnel, tearing his hands through his hair. "I lost my chance with you when I got banished from the domes."

"That wasn't your fault—"

"It doesn't matter." Kieran punched his fist into the wall. Tiny bits of rock clattered to the ground.

Nola ran to him, taking his hand in hers, expecting to see blood and broken bones. But his hand was perfect. The skin unharmed.

"See," Kieran panted. "I'm not who I used to be." He took Nola's face in his hands. "I love you, Magnolia Kent. I will always love you."

"Kieran, please don't." Pain dug into her chest.

"But I love you too much to let you stay down here in the dark." Kieran kissed her cheek. "And I love you too much to give you one night in a tunnel and send you away. You deserve the world, Nola."

He took her hand and turned down the tunnel, but Nola couldn't make her feet move.

"Kieran," she whispered, not waiting for him to turn back to her. "I love you, too. And I should have a choice."

His fingers tightened around hers, and together they walked down the tunnel toward 5th and Nightland.

Say something. There has to be something you can say to stay here. To stay with him.

They had nearly reached the metal door when a loud *thunk* echoed through the hall.

Nola stepped away from the door, expecting a burly guard to walk through. But the metal door stayed shut.

There was another *thunk*, and the noise from the club changed. The music silenced, replaced by frightened voices.

Thump.

The ceiling shook, sending a rain of dust down onto Nola and Kieran. More *thumps* came, breaking over the screams of the crowd. The door to 5th and Nightland swung open, and people poured out into the tunnel just before—

Bang!

The sound pounded into Nola's ears, blocking out the cries of the people around her.

Kieran grabbed her, shoving her against the wall and covering her with his own body as chunks of the ceiling came tumbling down.

There was more shouting and the sound of people running away down the tunnel.

Soon the shouts of fear vanished, replaced by roars of anger.

"Shit," Kieran muttered.

Nola looked up in time to see red beams of light darting through the dust of the ruined club.

Faint *pops* echoed through the air, and Nola watched the

shadow of a vampire fall before Kieran knocked her over, pinning her to the ground.

"Get out of our home!" a voice roared.

The screech of metal on metal wailed through the hall, followed by the sound of splintering wood and howls of pain.

The vampires were fighting back.

"Nola, I need you to run," Kieran said just loudly enough for Nola to hear his deadly calm voice. "I need you to run down this hall and not stop until you find where it meets up with the big tunnel. Go left from there, and you can find your way back to Emanuel's."

"You want me to get help?"

Another series of *pops* punctuated the shouts, but the vampires had armed themselves. This time, a guard fell to the floor. Another figure in a black uniform leapt into view, bringing down a heavy baton onto a vampire's neck.

"Help is already coming, but they can't see you here."

A *bang* shook the floor.

Nola watched in horror as the wall between the tunnel and Nightland began to collapse. Before Nola could gasp, Kieran had lifted her and was sprinting down the hall, carrying her in his arms.

He rounded the corner and held Nola to the side as a dozen vampires armed with swords, knives, and weapons Nola didn't recognize, ran past.

"Go," Kieran said. "Get where it's safe."

"Come with me!" Nola clung to Kieran's hand.

"They're invading my home, Nola," Kieran said. "I have to fight."

"I'll fight with you," Nola said, searching the floor for a rock, anything to defend herself.

"There are vampires in there," Kieran said, cupping Nola's face in his hands. "If you bleed, they could attack you. The guards can't see you. Just go. I'll meet you in the gallery when it's over."

He kissed Nola, quickly, urgently as shouts and the grinding of metal on metal came from the fight. "I love you, Nola. Now go!" he shouted over his shoulder as he disappeared into the dust.

Nola wanted to run after him. To shout at the guards to stop. These were people, too, and they had a right to protect their home. But if they saw her, they'd know she was a traitor, and the war with the domes would begin.

She stifled a sob and ran down the hall, half-blinded by her tears. Another group of vampires tore down the passage, knocking Nola off her feet. Pain shot through her wrist and ribs as she hit the ground. Spitting dirt from her mouth, Nola pushed herself to her feet, staring down at the hot sticky blood that covered her palm.

"Shit." She glanced up and down the tunnel. There was no one in sight, but a vampire would come soon. A vampire that could smell her fresh blood. Pulling with all her might, Nola tore the sleeve from her shirt. Grabbing a handful of dirt in her bleeding hand, she wrapped the leather around the soil, hoping it would be enough to cover the scent of her blood.

Nola ran down the hall, but the sounds of the fighting didn't seem to get any farther away. The guards had gained ground, delving deeper into Nightland.

How many guards had they sent that the vampires still hadn't —Nola couldn't stop herself from thinking—*killed them?*

Finally, she reached a door. It was metal but thankfully light enough for her to move on her own. Pain seared through her palm as she gripped the handle with both hands, forcing the dirt deeper into her wound.

As soon as she was through the door, she shoved it closed behind her. There was a lock on the inside of the door, a heavy metal bar that could be slid into place. It could block the Outer Guard from the hall—maybe only for a minute, but it would be something. But it would lock the vampires in with the guards. Shouts came through the metal door.

"Stay in formation. We don't leave without the girl."

Nola slammed the metal bar into the lock and stared at the door.

They were searching for her. If she let them find her, maybe they would leave. The fighting would be over. They had fought their way this deep into Nightland. The Outer Guard were stronger than Emanuel had thought.

But if they found out Emanuel had lied, they could destroy everything.

You can't be seen! Kieran's words pounded through her mind as the door shook.

Nola ran left down the corridor.

Please let me be right. If Kieran is hurt...

She pushed the thought out of her mind. He was a vampire. He only needed to protect his heart.

A woman stood in a doorway, clutching a sweater to her chest as she looked up and down the tunnel.

"Get inside," Nola shouted as she ran past. "The Outer Guard are here."

The slam of a door sounded behind Nola.

Her legs burned. How much farther until she reached Emanuel's house. Would she even be safe there? A group of vampires running in ranks, dressed all in black, charged past. Nola recognized Desmond's scarred, bald head as he ran in the lead.

Nola raced farther down the tunnel, where vampires still stood in the hall with no apparent concern for the attack.

"What's got the guards riled?" a man asked, stepping out in front of Nola. His long white fangs peeked over his bottom lip.

A human drinker.

"The Outer Guard," Nola panted, keeping her wounded hand clamped tight at her side. "They got into 5th and Nightland. They're coming."

The lights overhead flickered as though confirming her words.

"And the human runs," the vampire sneered. "Bloody and

weak." His eyes moved from Nola's panicked face to her injured hand. "I could protect you. The little girl lost in the dark."

He stepped closer, and the vampires around him shifted, forming a ring around Nola.

"Beautiful, weak, and so sweet," the vampire said, his black eyes gleeful. "You need protection. I could protect you. Make you mine." He leaned close to Nola, his fangs mere inches from her neck. The stench of sweat and stale blood wafted off his skin. He leaned closer, his nose brushing her neck. "You smell so pure, so clean."

"I am a guest of Emanuel," Nola said. "I am here under Emanuel's protection. And if you so much as touch me, Raina will have your head." Nola stepped back and stared unflinching into the vampire's black eyes.

"Raina." The vampire straightened.

"She owes me," Nola said. "Now get out of my way before the Outer Guard come."

The vampires stood frozen for a moment before, as a unit, they stepped back and out of her way.

Nola sprinted down the hall, the scent of the vampire still caught in her nose.

Soon, the doors became nicer, and she found the carved wooden door that led to Emanuel's home. Five guards stood flanking the entrance to the gallery.

"Nola." Bryant stepped forward as Nola skidded to a stop. "Where's Kieran?"

"At 5th and Nightland," Nola said as quickly as her panting would allow. "He stayed to fight. The Outer Guard made it through the doors. They're in the corridor."

"We know." Bryant opened the door to the gallery. "Get inside. They'll take you someplace safe."

Nola stepped into the gallery, and a cold hand closed around Nola's arm.

"And here I thought you might have run into the waiting arms of the guards," Julian said, dragging Nola through the gallery and to the living quarters.

"I thought about it," Nola said, her breath still coming in short gasps, "but I didn't know if it would make them stop. And Kieran said to stay out of sight."

"Kieran is a very smart lad." Julian led her through the kitchen and the narrow door in the back. There was a wooden door on the right and a heavy, metal door straight ahead.

Julian pounded on the metal door with his palm. "Dr. Wynne, I have Nola."

A shadow flitted behind a tiny piece of thick glass in the door. A creaking came from the other side before the door, even thicker than the entrance to 5th and Nightland, ground slowly open.

"Oh, thank God," Dr. Wynne said, beckoning Nola into the room.

"Reseal the door." Julian turned and ran away.

Dr. Wynne put his shoulder into the door and slid it shut before turning a thick metal wheel in the center that closed the lock with a heavy *clunk*.

"Where's Kieran?" Dr. Wynne asked as soon as the door had been secured.

"He's fighting," Nola said. A horrible stone of guilt settled in her stomach. "He told me to run. But there are others there. He'll be fine. He has to be."

"Nola dear," Dr. Wynne said, his voice unusually tired, "I gave up on my son being safe the moment I turned him into a vampire. It was my fault we were banished from the domes and my drug that turned him."

"To save his life."

"I saved his life by making him a part of a very dangerous community." Dr. Wynne took off his glasses and kept his gaze down as he slowly cleaned the lenses on his shirt.

Nola didn't miss the glimmer of tears in his eyes.

"Every day I have with him is an extra gift I don't deserve. Kieran is a brave man. He would never sit idly by while others are in danger. Of course he's fighting. And he won't stop until everyone is safe."

"But he'll be okay," Nola said, unable to keep a trace of question from her voice.

"He's a vampire, Nola," Dr. Wynne said. "And a strong one at that. That is the best assurance we have that he'll be back in a few hours. Beaten, bloody, maybe missing a few fingers. But he'll still be Kieran, and he'll heal."

"Because you made him that way." Nola turned to the door, wondering how long it would be until someone came for them.

"Because I made him that way."

CHAPTER TWENTY-FOUR

Nola scanned the room where she'd been trapped.

No. Protected. They're keeping you safe.

She had expected concrete, weapon-lined walls. But instead, a pattern of bright blue clouds decorated the eggshell-white walls. Along one side sat a small bed with a soft pink comforter, and in the corner Bea rested in a rocking chair, apparently unfazed by the commotion around her. Eden huddled at Bea's feet, clutching a ragdoll.

Of course Eden sleeps in the safest room in Nightland. Emanuel wouldn't have it any other way.

He's keeping me safe, too.

"How are you?" Nola asked, sitting on the floor.

"Good," Eden muttered, crawling over and planting herself firmly in Nola's lap. "Did you get a booboo?"

"A little one," Nola said, shaking her head at Dr. Wynne's startled look. "I fell and cut myself. It's not that bad. I just wanted to hide the smell."

Dr. Wynne pulled a wash basin and jug down from the dresser in the corner and sat on the floor next to Nola.

The walls shook, and Eden clung to Nola's neck. "It's okay,"

Eden whispered into Nola's ear. "My daddy made this place safe for me, and he'll come get us when he gets rid of the bad men."

"He sure will." Nola pushed Eden's curls behind her ears with her good hand, trying not to flinch as Dr. Wynne began washing the dirt from her other palm.

The walls shook again, and Nola swallowed hard, trying not to show Eden her panic. Trapped underground. What if the tunnel collapsed? They would be buried forever.

Nola tried to picture herself in the domes, full of light and air.

Far away from Kieran.

"Why did the bad men come?" Eden asked, standing up so she was eye to eye with Nola.

"They aren't bad men," Nola said. "You know how you're afraid of them? They're afraid of you, too. And sometimes when people are very afraid, they do things they shouldn't, and they hurt people."

"Why are they scared of me?" Eden tipped her head to the side and scrunched up her forehead.

"Because they don't understand how wonderful and precious you are," Nola said. "They don't understand your daddy is just trying to make a safe home for lots of people."

"If they did, would they go away?"

"I think so."

"When I get big, I will teach them we are nice, and my daddy is nice," Eden said, lifting her pudgy chin in determination.

"I'm sure you will."

"All done," Dr. Wynne said, tucking a bandage around Nola's palm. "While I admire the ingenuity of using dirt to try and cover the blood odor, I wouldn't recommend using tunnel dirt for that purpose in the future. It's not really sanitary. Although if it's either that or be considered a snack, I suppose the chance of infection is worth it."

"Right, desperate times only." Nola stood and sat on Eden's bed. The mattress springs creaked under her weight.

Eden followed her, curling up and tucking her head on Nola's lap. Another *boom* echoed through the walls, this one more distant than the last.

Were the guards being driven back, or simply coming at them from another direction?

Eden whimpered and covered her face with her doll.

"Hush," Nola said, stroking the girl's silky, black curls. "We're safe here. Just close your eyes and relax."

Nola hummed a song her father had sung to her when she was very little. She couldn't remember the words anymore. Only that she had liked the tune—the song had made her feel happy, safe, and sure her father would always be there to fight the demons away.

Nola kept humming as Eden's breathing became slow and steady, hoping Eden would fare better than she had. And Eden's father would come home.

Loud banging on the door shook Nola from her stupor. Eden clamped her hands over her ears. Dr. Wynne ran to peer through the glass slit in the door. Even Bea sat up straight in her rocking chair, the first sign she had given that she had noticed anything strange.

"Emanuel," Dr. Wynne said, opening the door and tripping over Eden as she streaked past him into her father's waiting arms.

Emanuel swept Eden up, holding her to his chest. "It's all right," he murmured. "You're safe, Eden. Daddy would never let anyone hurt you."

He had been in the fight. A long cut marred his cheek and blood matted his hair. The cut already appeared days old.

"Kieran?" Dr. Wynne said, before Nola could form the word.

"He's alive," Julian said from behind Emanuel's shoulder.

"Alive?" Nola clung to the door.

"He was hurt," Emanuel said. "Badly. But he'll heal."

"They didn't get his heart?" Dr. Wynne lifted a trembling hand to his glasses.

"No," Julian said, "though they tried their damndest. He's unconscious now, but I think if you give him another dose of ReVamp—"

"He shouldn't need anymore. Not for weeks." Dr. Wynne's voice sounded thin, like there wasn't enough of him left to contemplate the injuries of his only son.

"He needs to heal more quickly," Emanuel said. "Stitch him up, and give him an injection. Then we can wake him and get him to the bridge."

"Bridge?" Nola said. "What happened to Kieran that he needs more ReVamp? He's supposed to be able to heal."

"He will," Julian said.

"But—"

"Kieran needs to be fit for the exchange," Emanuel said. "We're moving forward."

"But they attacked us!" Nola said so loudly Eden covered her ears again. "They came in here and ruined everything, and you think they'll go through with the deal?"

"They'll have to," Emanuel said. "They won't leave you standing on the bridge."

"And you're just letting them take me?"

"They only sent in a handful of guards." Julian spread his hands in a helpless gesture. "If we tried to keep you here, it would be a rallying cry to start an all-out war."

"We can't protect Nightland if they decide to do that," Emanuel said, handing Eden to a waiting Bea who shuffled past them into the kitchen. "They could blast down from the city."

"It would be catastrophic, and not just for Nightland. For the humans who are still trying to survive aboveground," Julian said. "But after tonight, I can't find it in myself to believe the Outer Guard wouldn't do it."

"So, we go to the bridge." Nola's voice sounded far away as she said the words.

"I'll try and wake Kieran," Dr. Wynne said.

"Don't." Nola gripped his sleeve. "Let him sleep. He needs to heal."

"He would want to be there," Julian said.

Nola shook her head, wincing as the pain of heartbreak cracked in her chest. "I don't know if I have the strength to walk away from him." Her voice came out barely louder than a breath.

"Is there anything you want me to tell him?" Dr. Wynne asked, squeezing Nola's hand.

"Nothing that will make it hurt less."

CHAPTER TWENTY-FIVE

The tunnels had collapsed in places. Bits of stone and piles of dirt littered the corridor. Some of the light bulbs had blown out, and those that remained flickered feebly.

Raina maintained a viselike grip on Nola's arm as she steered her though the halls, half-lifting her over the ruble.

"I'm not going to try and run," Nola said as Raina's fingers dug painfully into Nola's arm when they passed a vampire lying in a pool of his own blood. The man's breath rattled though his wounded chest. "Should we help him?"

"He'll heal," Raina said. "And I'm not worried about you running. We have a lot of pissed off vampires who don't know if the Outer Guard are going to try and attack again. I'm supposed to get you to the bridge, and I'll be damned if I let someone snatch you before trade time. Sorry, you'll just have to live with the bruises."

Sour bile rose in Nola's throat as Raina led her past a woman mumbling and crying as she clasped her bloody stump of an arm.

They reached 5th and Nightland, but if Nola hadn't known their destination, she wouldn't have recognized the club at all.

No music pounded through the air. No dancers writhed to

the pulsing beat. The bright flashing lights had been replaced by pale moonbeams creeping in through the giant hole that led to the streets above. Lined up along one wall lay five vampires, their hands crossed gently on their chests. Nola tried not to look at the horrible wounds that covered their bodies. One woman had a hole larger than a fist in her chest. One man's head was barely attached to his neck. All were too far gone to heal.

Under the hole where the trap door to the street had been lay six guards, their bodies torn and beaten, their faces still hidden by helmets. The body of a tall, broad shouldered male lay farthest down the line. His boots were shiny and new, his uniform hardly worn aside from the tears from the fight.

"Jeremy." Nola wrenched her arm away from Raina and ran to the end of the line. She knelt next to the body and cradled his head, trying take off the helmet. Her hands shook too badly to manage even its slight weight.

"Let me," Raina said, lifting away Nola's trembling hands.

Raina pulled off the helmet, and tears streamed from Nola's eyes as a head of bright blond hair emerged.

Nola had seen this man before. He was just old enough to have always been in the class above her. Lying in the dirt, he looked like a child.

A surge of guilt flooded through Nola.

Not Jeremy. It's not Jeremy.

He hadn't been lost to Nightland. But someone would mourn when the blond boy didn't come home.

"Not him?" Raina asked after a moment.

"Not him." Nola pushed herself back up to her feet. "What are you going to do with them? They're Domers. They should be burned and scattered to the wind."

"After we get you traded back, we'll figure that out," Raina said, taking Nola by the waist and lifting her high into the air, passing her to hands that waited at street level. "If they play nice and give us what we asked for, we might give the remains back as a peace offering."

Desmond set Nola down on the cracked pavement.

"And if not?" Nola asked, giving a nod of thanks to Desmond.

"We put them in the river," Raina said. "It's where all the death around here comes from anyway."

"It's time," Bryant said from his place at the head of the pack of vampires that had assembled as Nola's escort.

Nola nodded, feeling more like she was being led to the gallows than sent home.

Bryant led them through the city. A haunting *clang* echoed down the empty streets every time he struck his pipe on his open palm.

The journey to the bridge seemed much shorter than the first time Nola had made the trek alone in the darkness.

As the bridge rose in the distance, a lone figure in a long, black coat emerged from the shadows. A silver sword peeked out from under the coat's trim.

"Nice of you to join us," Raina said.

"I was scouting the bridge, if you must know," Julian said as he matched step with Nola. "And they do seem to be playing nicely."

A strangled cough came from Raina. "We'll see."

The first gray of dawn peered up over the hill.

The shadow of the Outer Guard caravan waited across the river.

Nola stood flanked by vampires. Julian and Raina each held one of her arms.

"Just stay calm," Julian said in a low voice. "They want to get you home safe, and so do we. If we all stay calm, we'll be in the tunnels before daylight and you can have a nice breakfast with your loving mother."

Nola nodded, not trusting her voice.

"Don't play the victim just yet," Raina said. "Keep your big girl panties on until you get back to the domes. Then you can curl up in a ball and tell them how badly we abused you."

"I won't lie," Nola said. "You're not monsters. You never hurt me."

"They have to believe we kidnapped you," Julian said. "Don't worry about our image. Keep the story believable, just like we practiced."

"Besides, I stabbed you," Raina said, a glint of laughter in her eyes. "Use that for your inspiration."

"Right," Nola said. "That *did* really hurt."

"It's time," Desmond called from his perch on the side of the bridge.

"Forward ho," Julian said, pushing Nola in front of him and Raina as though using her as a human shield.

"Can't I walk next to you?" Nola said, fighting her instinct to run as guards piled out of the trucks.

"I want to get you home safe, dear," Julian said, "but I'd like to get home, too. And they're much less likely to shoot you than me. So, you first."

"Right." Nola put one foot in front of the other. But somehow the distance between her and the trucks never seemed to lessen.

I'll have to walk until dawn. We'll still be walking across this bridge when the sun rises and burns the vampires.

With a bright flash, all of the trucks turned their lights on as one, shining them directly at Nola. The hiss of the vampires echoed behind her. She tried to lift a hand to cover her eyes, but Julian and Raina kept her arms pinned to her sides. She squinted, trying to see past the lights. Spokes of bright white emanated from the sides of the glow that blinded her.

Shadows moved in front of the lights, and red beams joined the white ones.

"Lower your weapons," Desmond's deep voice boomed from far behind her. "Lower your weapons, Domers, or Magnolia Kent goes into the river."

The flashes of red lowered toward the ground.

"Magnolia, are you all right?" A magnified voice came from the far end of the bridge.

"Yes," Nola said, her voice stuck in her throat. She swallowed. "Yes!" She shouted.

"Bring the package to the middle of the bridge," Desmond called. "Once we confirm you've given us what we asked for, we'll give you the girl."

Lights bounced across the bridge as three guards ran forward, two with rifles pointed at the vampires, one with a box in his hands.

"That's it?" Nola asked. "That's all you wanted?"

"It's a lot." Julian let go of Nola's arm and took a step forward. "I'm coming to inspect the package."

Nola held her breath as Julian ran toward the rifles all alone.

"He shouldn't be out there by himself," Nola said. "What if something goes wrong?"

"Careful, Domer," Raina said, "you almost sound like you care."

The guards placed the package in the middle of the bridge and took three steps back.

Julian bowed to them as he reached the box before kneeling over it.

A minute ticked past and then another as Julian examined the package.

"It's all here," he finally called over his shoulder.

"Here we go." Raina pushed Nola forward. "Try not to end up in Nightland again."

"In case you stab me a little too well next time?" Nola asked, trying to sound cavalier as her knees wobbled with each step.

"If you hadn't been wearing an oversize protective guard coat, I would've gotten you in the heart. And then what would we have to trade?" Raina said.

Nola turned to see a smirk on Raina's face.

"Hooray for oversized coats," Nola whispered, unsure if any sound had really come out.

Julian stood, hands behind his back as he faced the guards.

"I'll pick up the box," Julian said. "Then Magnolia walks to you."

"The girl comes to us first," the guard said.

"Funny how I know our prisoner's name, and you call your citizen *the girl.*"

"Julian," Raina hissed.

"Anyway," Julian said, "I pick up the box, then you get *the girl* whilst we run away. If you don't agree"—Julian pointed over his shoulder, and instantly cold hands wrapped around Nola's neck —"one flick of my dear friend's wrists, and Magnolia is no more."

Silence hung over the bridge. Raina's fingers around Nola's neck drained the warmth from her body, leaving her shivering.

"I like that," Raina murmured. "Keep it up."

"Take the box," the guard said.

"Thank you." Julian lifted the box that seemed to weigh hardly anything, at least to a vampire.

"Now the girl," the guard called.

"Good luck," Raina said, shoving Nola forward.

Nola stumbled before her legs remembered how to walk. The bridge echoed with each step under the heavy boots Raina had given her. In two steps, she was past Julian. A moment later, a guard lifted her into his arms and sprinted back across the bridge, carrying her like a child.

Roars spilt the night as the Outer Guard's trucks started.

Nola twisted, trying to look back at the other end of the bridge to see if the vampires had made it to safety. In the glare of the truck lights, she could almost make out two figures running away across the bridge.

"You're safe now," the guard who carried her said.

"Is she hurt?" Lenora jumped out of the back of a truck and ran toward them.

Someone pushing a gurney sprinted forward.

Lenora grabbed her daughter's hand as the guard lowered Nola onto the gurney. Nola gagged as the smell of medicine and cleaner surrounded her.

Lenora gasped, looking horror-struck at Nola's red, scarred hands. "What did they do to you?"

"Out of the way, ma'am," a doctor said as two guards lifted the gurney into a truck. Lenora clambered in after, and the truck sped up the hill.

A guard waited in the corner of the truck. He reached out, placing a hand on Nola's shoulder before taking off his helmet.

Sweat covered Jeremy's forehead, and tears welled in the corners of his eyes.

"You're alive," he whispered, lifting Nola's hand to his lips. "Thank God you're alive."

CHAPTER TWENTY-SIX

The slow, steady beeping marked the minutes they forced Nola to lay in bed. After the Outer Guard raced her back to the domes, the doctors had made Lenora and Jeremy leave. They ran tests and scans, drawing her blood and searching her entire body for signs of harm.

"I'm fine," Nola said, so many times the words seemed to lose all meaning.

They put a mask over her face and made her breathe in medicine that smelled like soured fruit, then stuck needles into her arm to pump in antibiotics. Each of her bruises had to be recorded. Kieran's finger marks showed purple on her arms. The doctors all spoke in low voices about the horrible abuse she had suffered.

Nola bit her lips until they bled, fighting the need to scream that Kieran had been saving her life when he bruised her—he would never ever hurt her. But then they would know where Kieran was, and they would never believe her anyway.

Finally, when the sun had fully risen, the doctors left.

Before Nola could take a breath, more people invaded the bright white cell. Jeremy's father walked stoically into the room followed by a man with a bald head and thick black eyebrows, wearing a Dome Guard uniform. The embroidered rectangle on his chest read *Captain Stokes*. Lenora and Jeremy followed close behind, Lenora leaning on Jeremy's arm for support.

"How are you, Magnolia?" Captain Ridgeway asked in the softest tone Nola had ever heard him use.

"I'm fine," Nola said for the hundredth time that hour.

Captain Ridgeway nodded to Lenora and Jeremy, and they parted ways, taking up posts on either side of the head of Nola's bed as though guarding her.

Jeremy reached out to take Nola's hand, but it was heavily bandaged in thick foam. They had to heal the imperfections the rain had left on her skin.

Nola wanted to tear off the bandages and throw them to the floor.

Why does it matter if I'm not dome perfect?

"Magnolia," Lenora said, "did you hear him?"

Nola looked to Captain Ridgeway. He stared down at her with mixed concern and anger on his face. Nola hoped the anger wasn't for her.

"No," Nola said. "Sorry."

"I need to ask you what happened when they took you," Captain Ridgeway said. "The more we know, the sooner we can act."

"Act?" Nola tried to sit up in bed, but Jeremy's hand on her shoulder held her down.

"We need to know how they got in and what happened to you," Captain Ridgeway said, his eyes boring into Nola's as though he hoped to watch the events unfold within them. "The more we know, the better we can protect the domes and make sure the Vampers don't get in here again."

"All right," Nola said.

"They've said we can stay, if it'll make it easier for you. If you'll feel more comfortable," Lenora said, brushing a hair from Nola's face. She hadn't done that since Nola was very little.

"But if you would rather speak to us alone," Captain Stokes said, his glare darting from Lenora to Jeremy, "then I am sure they can wait outside and see you when we've finished."

Will it be easier to lie with them in here, or to say it all again later?

Jeremy's hand warmed Nola's shoulder. He was there, protecting her from his father and Captain Stokes.

"They can stay," Nola said.

"Fine." Captain Ridgeway nodded. "Now, start from the beginning."

"The beginning..." Nola's mind raced back to kissing Jeremy under the bushes. "I had a fight with my mother."

Lenora gave a sharp exhale. Nola looked up and found tears welling in her mother's eyes.

"I was upset, so I went to see Jeremy," Nola said. "I know it was late, and I shouldn't have been there—"

"I should have walked you home," Jeremy said, his voice a low growl.

"No." Nola laid a mittened hand on Jeremy's. She should have made them leave. She had only thought of making it easier on herself, not protecting them. "They wanted me. If you had been there, they would have hurt you."

"What happened when you left Jeremy?" Captain Stokes stepped forward.

"I was leaving, and then two people came out of the dark," Nola said, remembering the words Julian had taught her. "A man and a woman. The woman had a knife. She told me to send the guard at the stairs to Jeremy's house. She said she would kill me if I didn't. Her eyes were black. I knew she was a vampire and I wouldn't be able to run away, so I did it."

"What happened next?" Captain Stokes asked.

For the first time Nola noticed the recorder sitting in his palm.

"They made me put on the guard's hat and coat. We went back to Bright Dome, and in the back there was a loose section of glass. We crawled through it and into the rain."

"Did you move the glass or did they?" Captain Stokes asked.

Fingerprints. Julian had warned her once she told the guards how she had gotten out, they would check for fingerprints.

"I did," Nola said, "mostly. The woman told me to, and I tried, but it was heavy. The man ended up moving it in the end."

"What then?"

"We went outside. Down the hill toward the bridge. The rain was so thick, I could barely see. I got scared. I didn't know where they were taking me. So I ran. I barely made it ten feet. Something sliced into my back, and I fell. I think that's how I hurt my hands." Nola glanced down at the thick bandages that hid the red scars. "My head hurt, and when I woke up I was locked in a room. There was a doctor who took care of me. Then he came to ask me questions."

"Who's *he*?" Captain Ridgeway asked, a fire brewing in his eyes.

"Emanuel." Nola whispered the word. Julian had told her to say it, said to give the name, that the Outer Guard already knew who commanded Nightland, but the hatred in Captain Ridgeway's eyes frightened Nola.

Jeremy's hand tightened on Nola's shoulder. Had he heard of Emanuel, too?

"What did Emanuel want to know?" Stokes asked.

"About Green Leaf," Nola said, her stomach throbbing as her mother gave a tiny sob. "They wanted to know what seed groups you had brought back and if we were expanding the domes to accommodate planting the new crops. I was scared, and it didn't seem important, so I told him."

"Good girl," Lenora said. "Why on earth would they think you knew anything worth all of this?"

"I don't think they really cared," Nola said, keeping her words steady. "I answered Emanuel's questions, and he left. I didn't see anyone again until they came to tell me they had given you a ransom demand and you had agreed to the swap. A few times, they gave me food. But the next time Emanuel came to see me was for the trade. They put a bag over my head and took me to the bridge. I didn't see anything until the bridge was in sight." Nola looked to Stokes. "I'm sorry I can't be more helpful."

"You've done very well, Magnolia," Captain Ridgeway said.

"Dr. Kent, Jeremy, why don't you give us a few minutes?" Captain Stokes said, his tone brusque and hard.

"Why?" Jeremy tightened his grip on Nola's shoulder. "You've asked your questions. She needs to rest."

"I'm afraid there are a few things left unanswered," Captain Stokes said, "and I think perhaps it's better to leave Magnolia on her own to answer them."

"I'm not leaving my daughter," Lenora said. "Ask your questions."

"As you wish." Stokes nodded. "The doctors found traces of drugs in your system. A version of Vamp."

Lenora gasped and seized Nola's face in her hands, staring into her eyes.

"I'm fine, Mom." Nola sat up, trying to push her mother away with her mittened hand. "The doctor gave it to me. Just a tiny bit. He was saving my life."

"By trying to make you a Vamper?" Jeremy sat on the bed next to Nola, examining her eyes as though searching for a monster behind the blue.

"Vamp helps you heal faster," Nola said, touching Jeremy's cheek with her bandaged hand. "They don't have a hospital like we do in here. I was stabbed in the shoulder. I would have died. And I'm fine. I can eat food and everything."

"And your leg?" Stokes asked.

"I don't know how that happened," Nola said. "But the doctor said he did the same thing as with my shoulder. Is that all?"

Nola stared at Stokes who glanced at Captain Ridgeway before responding. "No. There are bruises on your arms."

"And they matter more than me being stabbed?" Nola said.

"They're hand prints," Captain Ridgeway said. "Marks like that, someone pinned you down."

Lenora grabbed Nola's arm with shaking hands and pushed back her sleeve. "Oh God."

Jeremy wrapped his arm around Nola, pulling her close to him. His angry breaths rattled against her cheek.

"What's your question?" Nola didn't let herself flinch as she met Captain Ridgeway's gaze. She had been pinned down. Kieran was trying to protect her from the Outer Guard's attack, but that had been after Julian had taught her the lie.

"How did you get those marks, Magnolia?" Captain Ridgeway asked. "We need to know who pinned you down. Did someone hurt you?"

"Did one of the Vampers attack you?" Stokes asked, stepping in front of Captain Ridgeway. "Did Emanuel force himself on you?"

"What?" Nola screeched. "No, why would you think that? I told you they kept me in a room."

"Where Emanuel visited you," Captain Ridgeway said. "It's not your fault, Magnolia. No one would blame you."

"Emanuel never hurt me," Nola spat. "He would never lay a hand on me."

"You were stabbed." Jeremy's face was ice white, pain wrinkled the corners of his eyes where laughter should have lived. "They *did* hurt you."

"Yes," Nola said. "No. Yes, I was stabbed. No, Emanuel never raised a hand to me. He never would. You talk about him like he's some kind of monster—"

"He's a Vamper."

"He's a leader!" Nola shouted, shoving her mother and Jeremy away. "He is a leader of a lot of very desperate people. Emanuel doesn't want to hurt anybody. He's just trying to help his people survive!"

"Then where did you get the bruises?" Captain Ridgeway asked, the angry lines between his brows the only sign he had noticed Nola's outburst.

"When your guards tried to destroy Nightland," Nola said. "When you decided to blow your way into the tunnels when you had already agreed to a deal. Emanuel had come to get me. There was an explosion nearby, and part of the ceiling in my room fell. Emanuel saved me. He knocked me down and pinned me to the ground, out of the way of the falling rocks. He didn't want me to get hurt."

No one spoke as all four stared at Nola.

"Magnolia," Lenora said when the silence had begun to pound in Nola's ears, "you should rest. I'm sure any other questions they have can wait until later."

"Yes, Dr. Kent," Captain Stokes said, "I'm sure we can speak more after Magnolia has regained her composure."

Nola laughed. "I'm sure we can."

"Come on." Jeremy took her elbow, guiding Nola to lie back on the bed.

"Dr. Kent, if I could have a word," Captain Stokes said, still not pocketing his recorder. "In my office."

Lenora looked down at Nola.

"Go, Mom. Get it over with so they can leave us alone."

"I'll be back soon," Lenora said, tucking the sheets in around Nola before following Captain Stokes from the room.

"You'll be safe here," Jeremy said. "I won't let anyone hurt you. Not ever again." He leaned down and kissed the top of Nola's head.

"There are guards in the hall," Captain Ridgeway said, his face softening. "You can sleep. The domes are secure."

"Thanks," Nola said.

Captain Ridgeway turned to leave, but Jeremy sat down next to Nola.

"Can I stay with you?" he whispered.

His father had stopped outside the door, standing guard, feet planted apart, one hand on his weapon.

"To see if I drool?" Nola asked. Her eyelids weighed as heavy as lead as she laid her head down on the pillow.

"To see that you're safe," Jeremy said, taking Nola's bandaged hand in his. "I almost lost you, Nola. I could have lost you forever." He kissed the inside of Nola's wrist. "I can't risk that again."

"I'm not going anywhere." Pain tore at the edges of Nola's heart as she said the words.

I have nowhere to go.

She couldn't leave the domes. Her future lay inside the glass prison. But as she drifted off to sleep, her mind flew to Kieran, lying in a hospital bed deep underground. And she knew he would be thinking of her, too.

CHAPTER TWENTY-SEVEN

Hurried whispers lured Nola back out of sleep. It took her a moment to realize the voices came from the shadows beyond her door.

"This is my fault, Dad." Jeremy dragged a hand over his short hair. "I should have protected her. I should have made sure she got home safe."

"You should have." Captain Ridgeway took his son by the shoulders. "You *should* have walked her home. You *should* have made sure she wasn't alone in the dark. Every day for the rest of your life you'll wish you had walked that girl back to her mother."

Jeremy clutched his chest as though someone had punched a hole straight through him.

"But it's still not your fault. There was no reason you should have thought Vampers would have found a way into the domes, let alone targeted Lenora Kent's daughter. Just because you *should* have walked her home," Captain Ridgeway said, still gripping Jeremy's shoulders, "that doesn't make what those monsters did your fault. That's on them, not you."

"It *is* on me," Jeremy said. "I could have stopped it. All of those scars are my fault. If one of those monsters raped her—"

"She says they didn't."

"She says they would never hurt her." Jeremy turned away from his father, and light fell across his face. His eyes were wide with madness and pain. "She thinks they're good people, Dad. What if they brainwashed her?"

"They didn't," Captain Ridgeway said. He turned to look in at Nola, and she clamped her eyes shut. "She's confused, but she's still her. It happens sometimes. Kidnap victims start to sympathize with their kidnappers."

"So, what do I do?" Jeremy said.

"Let her heal," Captain Ridgeway said. "Give her time to sort out everything those monsters put her through."

There was a long pause.

"And keep a close eye on her, in case she sorts things out the wrong way."

"Thanks, Dad."

"I always thought you'd be a good Outer Guard, Son," Captain Ridgeway said. There were two soft thumps of Jeremy being patted on the shoulder. "Between your mother's blood and mine, I knew you'd have what it takes. But now, I'll be damned if you don't turn out to be the best guard we've ever seen."

"Why?" Jeremy asked. His voice sounded closer, and his shadow fell across Nola's eyelids as he stood next to her bed.

"Because you've got that girl to fight for."

The doctors swarmed Nola as soon as she woke up. More blood to be drawn, more drugs to be administered. Lenora sat by her daughter's bed the whole time, asking questions about everything they were doing until Nola asked her to stop. She didn't want to know what the needles were for. She just wanted them to finish their work and leave her alone.

She hadn't seen Jeremy since she woke up. Every time she

thought of him, the guilt rushed back. He blamed himself for her being kidnapped, but that wasn't what had happened at all.

"Where's Jeremy?" Nola finally asked her mother when they took the horrible breathing mask off after a half-hour treatment.

"I sent him away." Lenora pinched the bridge of her nose. "He didn't sleep last night. He stayed awake, watching you. He's terrified you'll disappear again. I am, too."

"Mom—"

"I'm sorry we fought." Tears shone in the corners of Lenora's eyes. "You are a good and kind girl. You have a bigger heart than I am capable of, and if I had lost you—"

"You didn't."

"I know. And I am so very grateful for that." Lenora patted Nola's hand. The thick mittens had been replaced by green silicone gloves filled with goo that didn't seem to warm up no matter how long it touched her skin.

"And Jeremy," Lenora said. "He's a good boy. It's difficult for me to admit, but I was wrong about him. And his father. I don't think either of them slept while you were gone. If it hadn't been for Captain Ridgeway and the Outer Guard, I don't know if we would have gotten you back alive."

"Right. You're right."

Julian had taught her the lie.

He didn't teach me how to live with it.

"How's Sleeping Beauty?" Jeremy appeared at the door.

"I'm fine," Nola said.

I'm never going to get to stop answering that question.

"I thought *you* were sleeping," Nola said.

"I did." Jeremy smiled. "I'm bright as a daisy."

"If you're going to sit with her for a while..." Lenora said, standing.

"Go to your lab, Mom." Nola shooed her mother away.

"I'll check in later." Lenora gave a quick wave and slipped out the door.

"Wow," Nola said. "For her, that was downright clingy."

"She was worried about you." Jeremy sat down on Nola's bed, holding out a cup of foamy green sludge. "Terrified actually. We all were."

"So, now you want to poison me for scaring you so badly?" Nola sniffed the cup. It smelled like a mix between fungus, chlorophyll, and fertilizer.

"It's a detox shake." Jeremy grinned. "It's what the guards who go outside the domes regularly drink to help purify their systems."

Nola took a sip, and gagged on the thick froth.

"I never saw my dad with this." She tried to push the cup away, but Jeremy lifted it back to her mouth.

"He would have had it in the barracks, not at home. Drink up."

Grimacing, Nola took another sip.

"You'll be having this for meals for a few days."

"Lucky me." Nola took a gulp and regretted it instantly.

"You *are* very lucky." Jeremy took her face in his hands, leaning in so his forehead touched hers. "And I am very lucky to have you home."

"Jeremy."

"I thought, when the raid didn't get you"—Jeremy's hands shook—"I thought we'd lost you for sure."

"The Outer Guard," Nola said, freezing with the cup halfway to her mouth, "were they sent down to the tunnels to get me? Only to get me? Emanuel had already made a deal."

"We didn't think they'd show at the bridge, and we couldn't leave you with the blood suckers."

"But the guards. Six guards died." The air vanished from the room. From the domes. "And vampires. Vampires died, too. Because of me."

Her glass shattered as it hit the floor.

"No. Because of the Vampers that took you," Jeremy said.

"They took a citizen of the domes. We had to get you back. Those guards knew what they were getting into."

"Dead." The line of guards, their bodies torn and twisted, flashed through Nola's mind. "Bloody and dead because of me."

Sobs broke over her words. Gasping breaths racked her lungs, sending pain shooting into her heart. She had tried to help, and now there was blood on her hands.

Jeremy bundled her into his arms. Hushing softly, he lay back on the bed, cradling her to his chest. "It's all right, Nola. It's over now. I'll keep you safe. I love you."

CHAPTER TWENTY-EIGHT

It took two days for the doctors to allow Nola to go home. Two days of smiling sweetly and hoping no one looked too close. Jeremy stayed with her all the time, only leaving when Lenora came by for a few hours here and there.

Three times the doctors had retested her blood, making sure the level of Vamp had decreased. Making sure she hadn't been turned.

A full set of guards came to escort Nola home. Lenora held onto Nola's arm the whole way to Bright Dome, as though terrified Nola might crumble and fall. What Lenora should have been afraid of was the voice in the back of Nola's mind screaming, *Run!*

But how could Nola run when she was flanked by guards?

Nola could sense Jeremy's eyes on her back as they walked. He hadn't said anything about her breakdown in the hospital. Only sat with her as she stared at the ceiling, wondering if the bodies of the guards had been returned to the domes or dumped into the river. He'd made small talk about the planting and had given regards from classmates. But mostly he had just held Nola tight as though he feared she would shatter into a thousand irreparable pieces. He didn't know how right he was.

"Here we are," Lenora said when they approached the house, as though Nola might have forgotten what her home looked like in a week.

"Thanks for walking me," Nola said to the guards, looking at their boots instead of their faces.

"You're welcome, Miss Kent," one of the guards said.

Nola glanced up to the man's face. He was broadly built with a square jaw and bright blond hair.

"Your brother," Nola forced the question out. "He was at Nightland?"

"He was a brave man, miss," the guard said, the sudden crease between his eyes his only show of grief. "He died a hero's death."

"He did," Lenora said, taking the guard's hand. "And we are so very thankful."

The guard nodded to Lenora and looked back to Nola. "Welcome home."

Lenora kept her hand on Nola's back as she guided her into the house.

"Well," Lenora said as soon as she had closed the kitchen door, leaving only herself, Nola, and Jeremy in the house, "I guess I should make dinner. A nice welcome home meal."

"You don't have to," Nola said. "You can go back to the lab."

"No." Lenora shook her head, straightening Nola's braid over her shoulder. "I want to make you a welcome home dinner. Jeremy, you'll stay of course."

"Thank you, ma'am," Jeremy said.

"I think I'll go to my room for awhile," Nola said.

The clanging of the pots and pans drilled into her ears as she climbed the steps.

Nothing should be this normal. This calm.

Jeremy's footsteps followed her up the stairs.

"I'm fine," Nola said as she opened the door to her room. "I can find my..." but her words trailed off as she stared at her desk. A beautiful orchid waited for her.

"Do you like it?" Jeremy asked. "It's an old tradition. To bring your girl flowers."

"Where did you get it?"

Bright purple speckled the white petals.

"I have an in with the head of Plant Preservation," Jeremy said.

"It's beautiful." Nola turned to face Jeremy, feeling a genuine smile flicker across her face.

"Not as beautiful as you." Jeremy pressed his lips to the top of Nola's head. "I love you."

He had said it a dozen times since Nola came back. She still didn't know how to answer.

"Jeremy, I—" How could she begin to break his heart?

"Don't," Jeremy said, wrapping his arms around Nola. "I don't need you to say it back. I don't need you to tell me you want to spend the rest of your life with me."

Nola's heart stopped as Jeremy tipped her chin up to meet his gaze.

"But I need you to know that I love you. I've loved you for years, Nola, and if I hadn't told you before they took you, if you hadn't come back..."

"But I did," Nola whispered.

"And now I have the chance to tell you every day," Jeremy said. "I won't lose that."

Nola pulled her gaze away, looking back at the flower. The bloom seemed so strong, so sturdy, but a fierce wind could break its stem. Damage it beyond repair.

"I know you need time," Jeremy said. "You need time to sort through everything that happened. But I'll be here. I'll help you any way I can. I love you. I want to spend the rest of my life with you."

Nola's heart skipped. For a moment, she wasn't sure it would start beating again. For a moment, she didn't want it to.

"I'll wait for you, Nola. As long as it takes."

"But what if I'm not here?" Nola said.

Better to make a break. A clean break.

Jeremy froze his arms still around Nola's waist. "What you do mean *not here?*"

"I can't stay here. I can't stay in the domes." Now that she'd begun, the words tumbled out. "Eleven people died because of me. I can't stay locked in here and pretend it didn't happen. If I go out there, I could help people. There are gardens, ways to grow food out there. I could help people have food to eat. I could save lives. And then maybe those eleven deaths would mean something."

"They do mean something," Jeremy said. "Those guards who went down after you were trained. They were doing their jobs."

"They should have left me!" Nola clamped her hands over her mouth. "But they didn't. I'm here, and they're dead. And the only way I can live with that is to make my life worth it."

"You can do that here," Jeremy said, taking Nola's hands in his larger ones, making her newly healed skin disappear beneath his grasp. "You are brilliant, like your mother. You can join botany, help with the work of the domes."

"That's not good enough." Tears stung her eyes. "There are people dying out there right now, and I can't just pretend it isn't happening. I've seen it. I can't ignore it."

Jeremy studied Nola for a minute as though searching for a crack. "Fine. We'll leave the domes."

"We'll? Jeremy, no you don't understand."

"I lost you out there once. I won't do it again. I love you, Nola, and love means finding a way to stay together. You go out there, I go, too."

"Jere—"

"But not yet. You say you want to help people, and I understand that. But you haven't even finished school yet. You finish school and do your apprenticeship, then we'll go."

"An apprenticeship takes a couple of years. I can't stay here that long. There are people out there who need help now."

"There will always be people who need help, Nola. But how much more good will you be able to do when you're fully trained?"

Nola buried her face in Jeremy's shirt, shutting her eyes as tightly as she could bear.

"Once your training's done, we'll ask to be released from the domes." Jeremy held her tight, his broad shoulders surrounding her, blocking out everything else in the world. "I'll have a few years as a guard by then. I'll be able to protect you."

"Jeremy," Nola said, not taking her face from his chest. "I can't let you do that."

"You're not *letting* me do anything," Jeremy said.

"And when we get sick?"

Jeremy stepped back so Nola had to look at him. "I won't let that happen."

He meant it.

He would leave the domes for me. Leave everything he knows to follow me.

"I should go down," Jeremy said. "I don't want your mother to get worried about my being up here. She made a whole list of rules for me."

"She did?"

"Yep," Jeremy said. "And I'll follow them to a T. I don't want to lose my 'Nola privileges.'"

Nola took Jeremy's hand before he could leave. "How are you so good?"

"Because"—Jeremy leaned down, brushing his lips against Nola's—"I've spent a long time trying to become the kind of man you deserve." He smiled and disappeared through the door.

Nola went to the head of her bed, sinking down onto the floor. She took deep breaths, staring down at her perfect hands, trying not to let panic take her.

Jeremy loved her. He was perfect and good. He would do anything to keep her safe.

Kieran.

They had said their goodbyes. She should leave him alone. He didn't want her to be a part of Nightland, didn't want to make her a vampire.

Nola dug her fists into her eyes. Being a citizen of the domes meant making sacrifices to build a better world.

The figures of the dead eleven swam into her mind. The people who would morn for them, the days they would never get to live.

Nola reached into the desk drawer for a piece of paper. Her fingers closed around the tiny wooden tree Kieran had left for her.

Her hand shook as she found a pen and began to write.

Dear Jeremy,

I'm sorry. I'm sorry I'm not the girl you need me to be. I have to go now. I can't wait. I can't survive it. Please don't try to find me. More people will get hurt, and I can't survive that either.

Thank you. Thank you for being there even before I knew it was you holding me up. Please find another girl to love. Someone who can give you the life you deserve.

I love you, Jeremy. You are good, and brave, and everything wonderful. I will always love you.

Please forgive me,

Nola

She folded up the paper and tucked it under the orchid. He would find it first. He would tear apart the domes searching for her. Nola tugged on her work boots and pulled her thick coat from the closet, hiding the tree charm in her pocket. She could sneak out now while they thought she was resting. She would go to the atrium. Sneak onto a truck and find a way out from there.

Nola's mother's laugh rang up the stairs. She hadn't heard her mother laugh like that in years. The urge to run to her mother and hold her close froze Nola in place. But if she went down the stairs, she might never find the courage to leave.

Nola slipped the note back out from under the flower pot.

Please explain to my mother. And tell her I'm sorry.

She scrawled the words quickly and tucked the note back in place.

Taking the I-Vent from her drawer, she slipped it into her pocket. Eden might need it. Sitting on the windowsill, she swung one leg out the window.

BANG!

CHAPTER TWENTY-NINE

The sound shook the glass of the dome as brilliant orange flames lit the night. Nola tumbled backwards into the room, hitting her head on the floor. The ceiling spun as shouts shot up from the kitchen.

"Nola!" Jeremy shouted.

"What's happening?" Lenora screamed.

Jeremy threw open Nola's door.

"Are you hurt?" He knelt by her side.

"I fell," Nola said, shaking her head and sending her vision spinning again, "but I'm fine."

Flashing red light poured through Nola's window as the emergency siren blared to life.

"Is she all right?" Lenora ran into the room.

A piercing *beep, beep, beep* cut in between the siren's wails.

"We're under attack." The color drained from Lenora's face. "The domes are under attack. I have to secure the seedlings." Lenora looked down at Nola.

"I'll get her to the bunker," Jeremy said, yanking Nola to her feet. "You go."

Lenora nodded and ran out the door.

"Who's attacking us?" Nola screamed as another explosion shook the house. A fresh burst of orange lit the night, coming from the direction of the atrium.

"I don't know," Jeremy said, pulling Nola's arm. "But we have to go."

He ran down the stairs and out into the night, half-carrying Nola as she struggled to keep up.

Other figures dashed through the dark, heading for the tunnel. Nola couldn't recognize the people in the flickering shadows of the fire that blazed in front of the atrium. There were two bunkers for catastrophes in the domes. Nola had always thought they were for natural disasters—a hurricane strong enough to destroy their home—but now the Domers ran from monsters in the dark.

Tiny *pops* and *bangs* pounded through the glass as the guards added their weapons to the cacophony. At the base of the stairs Jeremy turned right, away from the atrium. The entrance to A bunker was there, under the vehicle site. But all the Domers ran away from the fighting, fleeing to the same hope of safety: the B bunker under the seed storage area.

Nola sprinted next to Jeremy, her feet pounding as quickly as they could. She stepped on something soft and tumbled to the ground.

"Nola!" Jeremy screamed, lifting her to her feet before she could see what she had tripped over. A man lay face down on the ground, blood pooling around him.

Jeremy pushed Nola against the wall as another group came running by, barely missing trampling the man.

"He's breathing." Jeremy hoisted the man over his shoulder. "We can't leave him here."

A *pop* sounded in the hall behind them.

"Go!" Jeremy pushed Nola in front of him.

Down more stairs and past the Dome Guard's quarters. The

doors to the empty barracks sat open. All of them had gone to the atrium.

Nola ran flat-out, Jeremy keeping up even with the added weight of the man.

They sprinted down another hall. A knot of people ran toward them. Nola moved to the side, letting them pass on their way to the atrium. The red lights flashed overhead, lighting the corridor and glinting off a head of scarlet and purple hair sliding out from under a hat.

"Raina!" Nola screamed.

Raina glanced back then picked up speed, running to the head of the knot of vampires, each wearing a heavily sagging pack.

"Stop!" Nola turned and tore back up the hall after the vampires.

"Nola, no!"

She heard Jeremy's shout but didn't slow down.

She sprinted up the stairs, ignoring the pain in her lungs, reaching the top just in time to see the last of the vampire pack round a corner toward the atrium. Nola pounded after them. People fled from the fight up ahead. Wounded guards were being carried into the hall, but there were still sounds of fighting coming from the atrium.

"Stop them!" Nola shouted to a group of guards that ran past her down to the tunnels Nola had just run out of, but the guards kept moving, their eyes focused front. Just before the atrium, the vampires turned left into the entrance for the small Grassland Dome.

Nola followed, barely hearing the shout of "Nola!" behind her.

The Grassland Dome had always been quiet and peaceful, filled with the rustling of grass. But tonight, screams rent the air. The explosion that had shattered the atrium had broken apart the glass here as well. A wide swath of the dome wall had shattered.

The vampires ran toward the break in the glass. In a moment, they would be outside. Nola couldn't catch them.

A group of guards ran in from the night, weapons raised high, blocking the way out.

Something hit Nola hard in the back, knocking her to the ground before a series of pops blasted over the bedlam.

"Stay down." Jeremy pinned Nola to the ground.

"Their bags." Nola shoved Jeremy off of her, trying to stand. "Their bags are full. They stole from us!"

Nola looked around wildly, half-expecting Emanuel to appear out of the dark and explain what was happening.

"I'll warn the guards." Jeremy leapt to his feet and charged toward the fight.

The guards battled hand-to-hand with the vampires now. Knives and clubs flashed in the night.

"Jeremy!" Nola screamed after him. The vampires would tear him apart. "Jeremy."

Nola ran after him, ignoring the sting as the tall grass tore at her legs. More vampires and guards had joined the fight, with more appearing from the darkness every moment. Jeremy charged toward the middle of it.

Nola ducked as a pipe flew from the hand of a fighter, whizzing only a breath away from her skull. A cold hand grabbed Nola's wrist, jerking her back.

Before Nola could look at the face of the man who had grabbed her, he knocked her to the ground, planting a knee in her stomach. The man smiled and bared his glistening white fangs that were already stained red with blood.

"Help!" Nola screamed.

The man laughed. No one could hear her over the chaos.

He leaned down, pinning Nola's arms to the ground. She screamed as his fangs pierced her skin.

"Get off of her," a woman shouted, and the man was torn from Nola and tossed aside like a ragdoll.

Nola grabbed the place on her neck where the man's fangs had been ripped from her flesh. Hot blood streamed down her collar bone.

Raina stood over her in the dark.

"That one is to be left alone!" Raina shouted at the man. "It's his orders."

But the man had already reached for his knife. Holding it high in the air, he threw the blade at Nola, bloodlust glinting in his eyes.

Nola saw the knife. Watched it flying end over end toward her heart. There was nowhere to run, nothing to do.

Raina leapt to the side, and the sharp point of the knife disappeared into her chest.

"No!" Nola shouted as Raina collapsed to the ground.

The man looked down at Raina's body and ran, cutting through the fight and out into the night.

"Raina." Nola crawled over to her.

The knife stuck out of Raina's chest, moving as she fumbled for the hilt. Raina coughed, and blood trickled out of her mouth.

"You're okay." Nola lifted Raina's head into her lap, pushing the scarlet and purple hair away from her face.

A trail of blood dripped from Raina's lips to her chin. She coughed again, and a horrible gurgling sound came from the wound.

"You can heal from this." Nola pushed her hands down around the blade, trying to stop the bleeding. "Should I leave the knife in or take it out?"

A shrill whistle came from outside the domes.

"It's too late for me, kid," Raina said, her voice crackling as she spoke. She coughed a laugh and smiled. "Funny that a knife stopped me."

"I'll get help," Nola said, laying Raina's head gently down. She stood, searching for a vampire who would know what to do. But all the vampires were running out through the glass. The guards who were left standing were still trying to fight, but there were too many vampires.

"Stop please!" Nola shouted. "She needs help! Raina needs help."

Only one of the fleeing pack turned to face her. He wore a dark hood, but as the red light hit his face, she saw him.

Kieran.

His eyes were coal black, no hint of green or gold left at all. He carried a heavy box in his arms and was surrounded by vampires holding weapons.

"Go!" a voice shouted. Bryant lifted his pipe and charged at the guards.

Kieran looked at her for only a moment longer before racing after him.

"Kieran," Nola whispered, sinking to the ground. There were more shouts of pain and a visceral scream.

"Jeremy!" Nola shouted.

He was in the center of the fight, trying to stop the vampires.

Nola turned back to Raina. Her eyes were closed, but she would heal. She had to. Nola wrenched the knife from Raina's chest and ran into the fight.

Jeremy's left arm hung limp and bloody at his side. In his right hand, he held a guard's club, which he swung at a boy with brilliant red hair.

Nola had seen the red haired boy in Nightland. He had looked so young and helpless in the tunnels beneath the city. Now he bared his teeth, violent hatred twisting his face. He swung his broken sword at Jeremy's neck. Jeremy jumped backwards, dodging the jagged strip of metal, and swayed sideways. He had stepped on a guard who lay face up on the ground, her eyes wide open and blank.

The red-haired boy lunged again, taking advantage of Jeremy's stumble. Jeremy tried to duck, but his wounds slowed his reflexes.

Jeremy!

Nola couldn't make her mouth form the word. She raised Raina's knife high in the air and sank the blade into the boy's back. The sword fell from his hand as he screamed in rage and pain before dropping to the ground.

He lay still next to the fallen guard, his eyes as blank as hers.

"Nola." Jeremy scrambled toward her.

"I know where the heart is," Nola said.

"Nola," Jeremy said, "are you hurt?"

"I know where the heart is." Nola turned away from the red-haired boy. He wouldn't wake up.

"We have to go," Jeremy said, pushing Nola to move with his good hand that still clutched the club.

They ran back out of the Grassland Dome. Blood slicked the corridor floor.

"We need to get you to the bunker." Jeremy turned toward the corridor that led to seed storage and safety.

Nola ran to the atrium instead, grateful that Jeremy's heavy footfalls followed her.

Most of the glass on the city side of the atrium had been shattered. Shards of it covered the ground. The vampires had fled into the night. Guards stood at the break in the glass, trying to secure their ruined wall, shooting at the vampires that fell behind the rest of Nightland's retreat. Bodies lay twisted and broken on the ground. A blond girl lay by the door.

"Nikki." Nola knelt next to her, not caring as the glass sliced her knees.

She placed a hand on Nikki's chest. Blood coated her pale pink shirt. Her throat had been torn out, and terror filled her unmoving face.

Nola kept her hand pressed to Nikki's chest, waiting for a heartbeat she knew wouldn't come.

"She must have tried to come to the atrium bunker." Jeremy lifted Nola's hand away.

The sounds of the fighting had ended, replaced by cries of fear and pain mixing with shouted orders.

"Guards on the break, keep watch!" a voice bellowed in the darkness.

"Dad." Relief flooded Jeremy's face.

"All others to the armory." Captain Ridgeway stood in the middle of the rubble. Blood covered half of his face, a gash still dripping on his brow. The stoic man who defended the domes had disappeared; a raging warrior now commanded the Outer Guard. "We're going after the Vamper scum."

Jeremy nodded and stood.

"What are you doing?" Nola grabbed his good arm as he moved to follow the others.

"Going with the guards."

"But you can't." Nola held tight to his hand. "You're hurt."

"I have to, Nola." Jeremy's voice was low, filled with an anger she had never seen in him before.

Nola wrapped her arms around him as he tried again to walk away. "You said we had to get to the bunker, so let's go. We'll go together."

"Gentry and my dad will both be out there," Jeremy said.

"They're both Outer Guard."

"So am I. I was sworn in the day they took you," Jeremy said. "It was the only way I could help find you. Nola, I have to go."

"What if you're hurt? What if—"

Jeremy leaned down, silencing her protests with a kiss. Nola wrapped her arms around his neck, pulling herself closer to him, desperate to keep him there with her.

"I can't lose you," Nola whispered as he pulled away.

"Never." Jeremy smiled. "I love you, Nola. I'll be home soon." He was gone before Nola could stop him.

CHAPTER THIRTY

Nola stood frozen in the sea of chaos, unsure of what to do. The guards would be going to Nightland soon. She knew more about the tunnels than any of them.

I can't let anything happen to Jeremy.

Nola ran to the front of the atrium. The shattered glass crunched beneath her feet with every step. Blood pooled on the floor in places. Boot prints smeared the red, leaving designs of death in the battle's wake.

Had the blood spilled from Domer or vampire veins? Was there even a way to tell?

The engines of the guard trucks had already rumbled to life.

"Wait!" Nola shouted as the guards loaded into the back. "I have to go with you!"

"Not a chance," one of the guards said, blocking her at the break in the glass.

"But I've been in Nightland. I can help." Nola watched the stream of uniforms filing out of the domes, wishing she could catch a glimpse of Jeremy.

"Miss, you're injured. You need medical attention."

Nola's hand flew to her neck, sticking to the blood that

covered her skin.

"The guards," Nola said. "Some of them are hurt, and they're going."

Gentry ran past, jamming on her helmet.

"Gentry!" Nola sprinted after her, catching Gentry's arm as she climbed into the truck. "I have to go with you."

"No citizens are to leave the domes, no exceptions," Gentry said. "Get to the bunker. Your mother will be there."

Nola took a breath, trying not to scream. Her mother waited below, guarding the seeds. But Jeremy would be in the tunnels.

Jeremy fighting Kieran.

"I can help. I know about Nightland!" Nola shouted desperately as Gentry turned away.

"If you think you have important information," Gentry said, "go to the Com Room. The operation is going to be controlled from there. Maybe they'll talk to you."

"Thank you," Nola shouted, already running for the far end of the atrium.

In the back of the atrium stood the tower, the only concrete structure to rise above the domes. Two guards flanked the doors to the staircase.

"I have to get up there," Nola panted, trying the push past the guards, who easily shoved her away.

"I'm afraid not, miss," the guard said. "Go to the medical unit. They can help you there."

"I'm Magnolia Kent. I was held in Nightland, and I have information that can help them. Please, you have to let me help."

One guard nodded to the other before raising his wrist to his mouth. "Magnolia Kent is here. She says she has information that can help."

There was a pause before a voice crackled out of the man's wrist. "Send her up."

"Thank you." Nola slid through the door before it had fully opened. She sprinted up the staircase.

This area hadn't been touched by the attack. The vampires hadn't bothered to break into the Communications Center.

Nola pounded up the flights of stairs, adrenaline pushing her to run faster.

How long until Jeremy reaches Nightland?

A guard waited at the top of the stairs, punching the code in to open the door only when Nola stopped, gasping for air, on the top landing.

"In here." The guard ushered Nola into the wide room.

She had been in the Com Room only once before. Years ago. Her entire class had been brought up here to see how communication with the other domes and the rest of the outside world worked. That day, the room had been a place filled with wonder, where she could see the face of a person on the other side of the world as they spoke. That day the world had seemed infinite and wonderful.

Today, chaos filled the tower.

Happy faces weren't smiling back from the screen. Instead, a live feed of the guards on their way to Nightland took up the whole wall. The Outer Guard poured out of their trucks onto the street at 5th and Nightland.

"Magnolia." Captain Stokes limped toward her. "They said you have information."

Nola's mind flickered back to her lessons with Julian. Sitting at the table, learning the things she was allowed to say.

The lie doesn't matter anymore. Nightland destroyed my home.

"I know where in Nightland Emanuel lives," Nola said. "I can tell your men how to get there."

Stokes stared at her for a moment. "Do it."

"But there's a little girl," Nola said as a man strapped a headset on her. "You have to promise me you won't hurt the little girl."

"We aren't the monsters here," Stokes said. "We don't hurt children."

The Outer Guard were in Nightland now.

"Tell them which way." Stokes fixed his gaze on the screen.

Nola squinted at the picture, trying to make sense of the shadows. "The second tunnel on the left, the one with the door blown off. Go that way."

The guards all moved in formation, slowly and methodically sweeping their lights in the tunnel. As the beams flashed over the rubble, Nola remembered the last time the guards had been in Nightland. Kieran had protected her, and now she was sending the guards after him.

"How far down?" Stokes asked.

Nola swallowed and looked out over the atrium. Smoke still billowed from the fire below. Through it she could barely see the dome helicopters taking flight. The helicopters had no sides. No defense against attack. But the brave pilots would fly over the city to try and aid their compatriots. They were going to help Jeremy.

"They'll hit a bigger tunnel. Follow that left until they find the wooden door," Nola said, her voice a harsh whisper. "It's old, and the wood has carvings in it. Go through there to the gallery. It's like an old library." Nola waited, watching the screen.

Screams carried through the feed.

"Behind you!" a man's voice shouted.

"I've got him!" a woman answered.

A *pop* and a scream of rage flooded Nola's ears as the screen flashed and went black.

"There are more behind him!" a voice shouted. "Keep going. We'll cover you."

The sounds of labored breathing and more shouting pounded into Nola's ears.

"I think I found it," the voice said after a moment. "Yep, this is it."

"We're clear," a different voice said.

"Where now?"

"Go through the door at the end," Nola said. "There's a kitchen on the right. In the back, there's another door. Through there is a heavy metal door. It's the safe room. That's where Emanuel will be."

"How do you know?" Stokes turned to Nola, his eyes sharp even though blood dripped from his leg.

"That's where his daughter will be," Nola said. "He wants to keep her safe."

"We're in the kitchen," the voice came through the headset. "The room is empty. The room with the metal door is open."

"Emanuel left." The words felt hollow in Nola's mouth.

"What?" Stokes said.

"Emanuel left," Nola said. "If Eden is gone, he will be too."

"How do you know?" Stokes asked, his forehead so furrowed his eyebrows had become one angry strip of black.

"The garden." Nola pointed out the window to the skyline of the city. "On the roof above Nightland, the second tallest building in the city, there should be a garden on the roof." Just because Emanuel left didn't mean all of Nightland was gone. Maybe Kieran had stayed behind in the city, saving the poor and the hungry.

The guard barked orders for a helicopter to circle the building.

Nola watched the light of the helicopter circling in the air. It looked like a fairy, far away over the city. Barely even a speck in the distance.

"There's a bunch of trash on the roof, sir," the pilot's voiced crackled in her ears. "It looks like there was something here, but whatever it was, it's gone now."

Nola's heart crumpled. The static of the screen swayed in front of her. "They're gone."

The garden, Dr. Wynne, Kieran.

"He's gone."

Nola's knees buckled. Arms steadied her and lifted her to a chair. But she couldn't think, couldn't move beyond Kieran.

Gone.

CHAPTER THIRTY-ONE

They sat her in a chair in the back of the Com Room. A doctor came up and cleaned and wrapped the wound on her neck.

"You're a lucky girl," the doctor said. "If you'd torn your jugular, there's nothing we could have done."

"Raina saved me." Nola stared at the dried blood that still covered her hands.

Mine, Raina's, the red-haired boy I killed, Nikki's. Who else's?

She couldn't even remember.

"Magnolia." Stokes came over from the giant screen. He had been shouting into the com a few minutes ago. Vampires had been hiding in the tunnels, waiting to ambush the guards. The guards kept talking about Emanuel leaving traps. But Emanuel would be out of the city by now, finding cover before dawn.

"Magnolia," Stokes said. "I need to ask you some questions."

"She needs to rest," the doctor said, planting himself in front of Nola.

She wanted to thank him, but Stokes had already pushed the doctor out of the way.

"I have guards risking their lives in the city," Stokes said. "She can rest when they do."

The doctor looked as though he might argue for a moment before shaking his head and walking through the metal door to the stairs.

Nola wanted to follow him. But where would she go? Had her mother made it home yet? Was her house even still standing? Had Bright Dome been destroyed?

"How did you know the path through the tunnels?" Stokes asked.

"He walked me from 5th and Nightland, from the Club to the gallery," Nola said. "He wanted me to see where he lived."

"And the garden on the roof?"

"He took me up." Tears burned in the corners of Nola's eyes. "He wanted to show me what they had built. He said they were finding a way to feed the city."

"Why didn't you tell us?"

"He said not to," Nola said. The burning had moved to her throat. "He said you would destroy the food, and people would starve. I thought they only wanted the ransom. I thought it was over and I would never see him again. He said they wanted to be left alone. I didn't want more fighting." Tears streamed down Nola's face.

"Sir," a man shouted from the front of the room. "We have a problem. The convoy's been attacked at 10th and Main."

Stokes cursed and ran back to the screen.

"We have wounded!" a voice echoed over the com. "We need emergency medical assistance."

Guards tore around the room, calling everyone they could for help. Nola pushed herself to her feet and stumbled to the door, running from the room before anyone tried to call her back.

Guards sprinted up and down the stairs. What had happened on the street? Sour rose into Nola's throat.

Wolves. There are still werewolves on the streets.

Back in the atrium, guard trucks drove in and out of the break in the glass, ignoring the place where the ruined door had been. Doctors rushed to the injured.

Nola watched as uniforms ran past, searching for Jeremy in the throng.

She shoved her shaking hands into her coat pockets. Her fingers closed around the tiny tree.

A truck rolled in, and gurneys were pulled from the back, but the doctors walked straight past. Those guards had been covered in white sheets. The doctors couldn't do anything for the dead.

Nola stood still as the chaos moved around her, her eyes constantly searching for Jeremy in the crowd. Every time a gurney passed, her heart stopped.

Not Jeremy. Please, not Jeremy.

Her nails dug into her palm as she gripped the tree. The wood cracked in her grasp. She pulled her hand from her pocket to stare at the broken and blood-covered charm. Tipping her palm, she let the tree tumble to the floor. The wood disappeared in the sea of shattered glass and blood.

The sky had turned from gray to pale orange as the sun began to rise, then back to gray as dark clouds coated the horizon. Trucks scrambled back out to the city. They had to get the rest of the guards inside before the rains began.

Lightning split the sky in the distance. The rumble of thunder shook the broken glass.

Another truck pulled into the dome. There were no gurneys this time. Only guards carrying their injured fellows.

"That's the last one!" the driver called just as the rain began to patter against the dome.

Nola ran toward the truck. Jeremy had to be in there. He had to be in the back of the truck. Nola scrambled into the truck bed. Blood stained the empty seats. "Jeremy."

She jumped down from the truck, stumbling before running through the crowd. "Jeremy! Jeremy!"

The bodies draped in white had been lined up against the wall, waiting for the families to be notified and the grieving to begin.

"Miss, you can't be over here," a guard said as Nola swayed staring at the bodies.

"Jeremy Ridgeway." Her mouth was dry. She could barely form the words. "Is he—"

"Nola," a voice called from behind her.

Nola turned to see Jeremy running toward her.

"Jeremy." Before she could remember how to move she was in his arms. She wrapped her arms around his neck so her toes barely touched the ground, pressing her cheek to his, feeling his warmth pass into her.

Tears streamed down her face as she sobbed, the exhaustion and pain of the horrible night finally flooding through her.

"Shh," Jeremy whispered. "I'm here."

"I thought," Nola coughed, "I thought I'd lost you. I waited, and I looked for you, but you didn't come back in the trucks. I thought you were gone."

Jeremy pulled away, looking down into Nola's eyes. "I would never leave you, Nola."

She leaned in, pressing herself to him as she kissed him. The world spun, but he held her close, keeping all she had been from slipping away.

Thunder shook the air again.

The rain pounded down on the dome, pouring through the break in the glass in solid sheets.

"What are we going to do?" Nola asked.

The guards backed away from the break, watching helplessly as contamination violated their home. But there was no way to fight the rain.

"We salvage what we can," Jeremy said, still holding Nola close. "Then we rebuild, we move on."

"We move on."

Jeremy took Nola's hand, and she didn't argue as he led her

away from the atrium. Through the broken dome and past the broken bodies. Down the corridor to Bright Dome. Back home. There was nowhere else to go now.

Nola's journey continues in Boy of Blood.
Order your copy now.

NOLA'S JOURNEY CONTINUES IN BOY OF BLOOD

CHAPTER 13.5

Two Weeks Before Nightland's Attack

"Moving the plants is taking more time than was allocated." Lenora Kent stood in front of the giant screen in the Com Room, her chin tipped up and hands planted on her hips.

"Why?" The image of Dr. Marcum leaned in.

Captain Ridgeway gazed down at his hands resting on his knees. He didn't need to watch Lenora's grand show of bristling at being questioned. He'd witnessed the display too many times before. He had better things to be doing than sitting with the rest of the Domes Council staring at a screen, but the Incorporation had summoned them.

The Incorporation rules us all.

"The work we're doing is delicate," Lenora said. "I made it clear at Green Leaf that I would need extra hands in moving the plants to make room for the new rain forest additions."

"A request which we granted," Dr. Marcum said.

"I thought," Lenora said, "you would be sending me people trained in botany, not letting the children out of school to run amok with my plants."

Captain Ridgeway glanced back to the screen as curiosity won out. If Dr. Marcum took offense to Lenora's tone, he didn't show it.

"I'm supervising teenagers," Lenora said. "I can't do any of the work myself. I'm too busy making sure none of the students I've been given destroy the plants that feed the population of these domes. If the Incorporation won't send workers from other domes to help with the process, then you have to choose. Do you want the work done quickly or done well?"

Dr. Marcum nodded for a moment before speaking. "I appreciate your situation, but the Incorporation doesn't have the means to ship workers from one location to another. Moving the new specimens is enough of a strain on our resources."

Lenora glared at the screen.

Any other department head from the Incorporation wouldn't have stood for such defiance. But Captain Ridgeway didn't even bother to hope Lenora would finally be told orders were orders and figuring out how to get the work done was a part of being trusted with the leadership of their domes.

"I can delay the shipment of the new rain forest assets by a week," Dr. Marcum said. "Any longer would put the plants at risk."

"Thank you, Dr. Marcum," Lenora said. "We'll have the dome ready to receive our new arrivals."

Captain Ridgeway looked away from the giant screen and to the wide window that faced the city. No smoke rose in the cloudless sky. The smog levels hadn't been high enough to cause real concern when he sent the morning patrol across the bridge to monitor the streets. No one had called him with word of any new food riots or violence of any kind since daybreak.

A small part of him wished a Vamp lab would catch fire. Just a bit of black smoke on the horizon and he'd have an excuse to leave the meeting.

"Captain Ridgeway," a grating voice came through the screen.

The captain scanned the city for smoke one last time before

standing up and taking Lenora's place in the center of the Com Room.

"Commander Salinger." Ridgeway gave a slow nod that bordered on a bow.

Salinger didn't prompt Ridgeway to speak. He might as well have been a bald, long-limbed statue placed in Incorporation Headquarters.

"The dangers in the city are escalating," Captain Ridgeway said. "The pure human population is practically extinct at this point."

"Extinct?" Salinger said.

"Between Vamp and Lycan, there are barely enough unchanged adults to work in the factories," Ridgeway said. "In the past week, we've had to raid two factories that had resorted to hiring Vampers as workers."

"Disgusting."

Ridgeway didn't look behind him to see which of the Dome Council members had spoken.

"By our estimation, the number of changed residents in the city is well into the thousands," Ridgeway said.

Salinger's pale eyebrows pinched together.

Another figure stepped onto the screen. "Are you telling us that there are thousands of potential combatants in your city?" Dr. Ray, the head of Incorporation assets, said.

"Yes, ma'am." Ridgeway gave another slow bow-like nod. "I've been warning the Incorporation of this possibility for months."

"In all other dome locations, drug users have been killing each other off as quickly as newly changed have been created," Dr. Ray said. "We've always seen stability in the Vamper populations."

"If you'll review my report," Ridgeway said, "you'll see Lycan is encouraging the formation of packs. Large groups of users that flock to an alpha leader. These packs are a massive risk to my guards."

"That still doesn't account for—" Dr. Ray began.

"How are the Vampers not slaughtering each other?" Salinger said. "The population should be held steady by the availability of human blood to drink and territory to claim."

"My patrols have come to believe that there's a Vamper nest in the city," Captain Ridgeway said. "According to our sources, there is a group of upwards of a thousand Vampers who have banded together."

The sounds of his fellow Council members stirring rustled behind him.

"If a force even a few hundred strong attacked my Outer Guard on the street," Ridgeway said, "Commander, it would be nothing less than a slaughter."

"That is the risk the Outer Guard take," Captain Stokes said.

Ridgeway locked his arms at his sides, refusing to acknowledge Stokes.

"If there are a full thousand combatants hiding in the city," Ridgeway said, "and that group chooses to cross the river and attack, in our current state we cannot defend the domes."

"An attack on the domes falls under the realm of the Dome Guard," Captain Stokes said, "not the Outer Guard."

"The Dome Guard don't have the training, experience, or capability to repel an attack on the domes," Ridgeway said. "We can pretend otherwise, but if the worst comes, it will be my people fighting at the front, and we all know it."

"How dare—"

Salinger raised his hand, silencing Stokes.

"It would fall to the Outer Guard," Salinger said. "And from the sound of it, Captain Ridgeway, you yourself don't believe your people capable of defending your home."

"My guards are capable," Ridgeway said, "but we're fighting Vampers and wolves who can be shot in the stomach and not die."

"Are you asking for the Incorporation's assistance in remedying the matter?" Salinger said.

A shiver ran down Ridgeway's spine.

"There are resources being produced in the city that are still very useful to the domes," Dr. Ray said.

"I am confident in the ability of my guards to defend these domes without the assistance of the Incorporation," Ridgeway said.

Dr. Ray's shoulders relaxed.

"What I am asking for," Ridgeway said, "is approval to move forward with the alternatives we have discussed."

The scraping of chairs as the council members behind him shifted in their seats set his teeth on edge.

"My Outer Guard are battling Vampers and wolves every night," Ridgeway said. "What I'm asking is for you to give them a chance to survive."

Salinger raised a hand, muting the video. He turned his back to the screen, speaking to the out of sight members of the Incorporation board.

"This is wrong," Lenora said. "We all know it. The domes were built to—"

"To survive the end of the world." Ridgeway rounded on her. "I am finding a way for my men, for all of us, to survive."

"My husband was an Outer Guard for years. He fought in the city," Lenora said. "He never would have stooped so disgustingly low."

"Your husband died on the streets," Dr. Mullens said. "I, for one, am tired of Outer Guard corpses being carried back into the domes. It's my job to keep our people healthy. If we have to take extreme measures, so be it."

Lenora shook her head, biting her lips together as though for once choosing to swallow her words.

A *ding* rang from the screen as sound returned.

"You have the Incorporation's blessing to proceed," Salinger said.

"Thank you, Commander." Ridgeway bowed. "You've just saved a lot of lives."

"Protect the domes at all costs," Dr. Ray said. "The assets in the domes are more valuable than what the city still has to offer."

"Of course, Dr. Ray," Ridgeway said.

"If you fail to secure the city," Salinger said, "I will have no choice but to personally intervene. Do not allow the liberties the Incorporation has granted to have been in vain."

The surge of triumph that had lifted Ridgeway's chest vanished. "Commander, I am confident my guards will be able to protect the domes. You've granted us the gift we've been waiting for. Graylock will turn the tide of this war."

What secrets hide in the domes? Find out in Boy of Blood.

ESCAPE INTO ADVENTURE

Thank you for reading Girl of Glass. If you enjoyed the book, please consider leaving a review to help other readers find Nola's story.

As always, thanks for reading,

Megan O'Russell

Never miss a moment of the danger or romance.

Join the Megan O'Russell mailing list to stay up to date on all the action by visiting https://www.meganorussell.com/book-signup.

ABOUT THE AUTHOR

Megan O'Russell is the author of several Young Adult series that invite readers to escape into worlds of adventure. From *Girl of Glass*, which blends dystopian darkness with the heart-pounding danger of vampires, to *Ena of Ilbrea*, which draws readers into an epic world of magic and assassins.

With the *Girl of Glass* series, *The Tethering* series, *The Chronicles of Maggie Trent*, *The Tale of Bryant Adams,* the *Ena of Ilbrea* series, and several more projects planned, there are always exciting new books on the horizon. To be the first to hear about new releases, free short stories, and giveaways, sign up for Megan's newsletter by visiting the following:

https://www.meganorussell.com/book-signup.

Originally from Upstate New York, Megan is a professional musical theatre performer whose work has taken her across North America. Her chronic wanderlust has led her from Alaska to Thailand and many places in between. Wanting to travel has fostered Megan's love of books that allow her to visit countless new worlds from her favorite reading nook. Megan is also a lyricist and playwright. Information on her theatrical works can be found at RussellCompositions.com.

She would be thrilled to chat with you on Facebook or Twitter

@MeganORussell, elated if you'd visit her website MeganORussell.com, and over the moon if you'd like the pictures of her adventures on Instagram @ORussellMegan.

ALSO BY MEGAN O'RUSSELL

The Girl of Glass Series

Girl of Glass

Boy of Blood

Night of Never

Son of Sun

The Tale of Bryant Adams

How I Magically Messed Up My Life in Four Freakin' Days

Seven Things Not to Do When Everyone's Trying to Kill You

Three Simples Steps to Wizarding Domination

Five Spellbinding Laws of International Larceny

The Tethering Series

The Tethering

The Siren's Realm

The Dragon Unbound

The Blood Heir

The Chronicles of Maggie Trent

The Girl Without Magic

The Girl Locked With Gold

The Girl Cloaked in Shadow

Ena of Ilbrea

Wrath and Wing

Ember and Stone

Mountain and Ash

Ice and Sky

Feather and Flame

Guilds of Ilbrea

Inker and Crown

Myth and Storm

Heart of Smoke

Heart of Smoke

Soul of Glass

Eye of Stone

Ash of Ages

Made in the USA
Coppell, TX
18 July 2021

59145046R00142